SUMMER LOVIN'

Praise for Julie Cannon

Shut Up and Kiss Me

"A feel good, tingly romance."—*Best Lesfic Reviews*

"Fast-paced, sexy, and fun with a bit of an insta-love plot (a trope I love!) I thoroughly enjoyed this read."—*JK's Blog*

"Great story, and I will definitely read this author again!"—*Janice Best, Librarian (Albion District Library)*

Wishing On a Dream—**Lambda Literary Award Finalist**

"[The main characters] are well-rounded, flawed and with backstories that fascinated me. Their relationship grows slowly and with bumps along the way but it is never boring. At times it is sweet, tender, and emotional, at other times downright hot. I love how Julie Cannon chose to tell it from each point of view in the first person. It gave greater insight into the characters and drew me into the story more. A really enjoyable read."—*Kitty Kat's Book Review Blog*

"This book pulls you in from the moment you pick it up. Keirsten and Tobin are very different, but from the moment they get together, the heat and sexual tension are there. Together they must work through their fears in order to have a magical relationship."
—*RT Book Reviews*

Smoke and Fire

"Cannon skillfully draws out the honest emotion and growing chemistry between her heroines, a slow burn that feels like constant foreplay leading to a spectacular climax. Though Brady is almost too good to be true, she's the perfect match for Nicole. Every scene they share leaps off the page, making this a sweet, hot, memorable read."—*Publishers Weekly*

"This book is more than a romance. It is uplifting in a very down-to-earth way and inspires hope through hard-won battles where neither woman is prepared to give up."—*Rainbow Book Reviews*

I Remember

"Great plot, unusual twist, and wonderful women…an inspired romance with extremely hot sex scenes and delightful passion." —*Lesbian Reading Room*

Breaker's Passion

"[A]n exceptionally hot romance in an exceptionally romantic setting…Cannon has become known for her well-drawn characters and well-written love scenes."—*Just About Write*

"Cannon writes about Hawaii beautifully, her descriptions of the landscape will make the reader want to jump on the first plane to Maui."—*Lambda Literary Review*

"Julie Cannon brilliantly alternates between characters, giving the reader just enough backstory to entice, but not enough to overwhelm. Cannon intertwines the luscious landscape of Maui and its tropical destinations into the story, sending the reader on a sensuous vacation right alongside the characters."—*Cherry Grrl*

Descent

"If you are into bike racing, you'll love this book. If you don't know anything about bike racing, you'll learn about this interesting sport. You'll finish the book with a new respect for the sport and the women who participate in it."—*Lambda Literary Review*

"Julie Cannon once again takes her readers somewhere many have not been before. This time, it's to the rough and tumble world of mountain bike racing."—*Just About Write*

Power Play

"Cannon gives her readers a high stakes game full of passion, humor, and incredible sex."—*Just About Write*

Just Business

"Julie Cannon's novels just keep getting better and better! This is a delightful tale that completely engages the reader. It's a must read romance!"—*Just About Write*

Uncharted Passage

"Cannon has given her readers a novel rich in plot and rich in character development. Her vivid scenes touch our imaginations as her hot sex scenes touch us in many other areas. *Uncharted Passage* is a great read."—*Just About Write*

Heartland

"There's nothing coy about the passion of these unalike dykes—it ignites at first encounter and never abates...Cannon's well-constructed novel conveys more complexity of character and less overwrought melodrama than most stories in the crowded genre of lesbian-love-against-all-odds—a definite plus."—*Richard Labonte, Book Marks*

"Julie Cannon has created a wonderful romance. Rachel and Shivley are believable, likeable, bright, and funny. The scenery of the ranch is beautifully described, down to the smells, work, and dust. This is an extremely engaging book, full of humor, drama, and some very hot, hot sex!"—*Just About Write*

Heart 2 Heart

"*Heart 2 Heart* has many hot, intense sex scenes; Lane and Kyle sizzle across the pages. It also explores the world of a homicide detective and other very real issues. Cannon has given her readers a read that's fun as well as meaty."—*Just About Write*

By the Author

Visit us at www.boldstrokesbooks.com

SUMMER LOVIN'

by
Julie Cannon

2021

SUMMER LOVIN'

ISBN 13: 978-1-63555-920-0

This Trade Paperback Original Is Published By
Bold Strokes Books, Inc.
P.O. Box 249
Valley Falls, NY 12185

First Edition: July 2021

Credits
Editor: Shelley Thrasher
Production Design: Stacia Seaman
Cover Design by Jeanine Henning

After the year we've had, we all need some summer fun. Enjoy!

Prologue

All right, ladies. What have you decided?" Addison Bradbury looked at the two women sitting around the table at the far end of her office.

"I'll start."

Cora Donaldson, the head of purchasing, spoke first. She had been at Bradbury Construction for seven years, one of the first people Addison hired when she took the reins of her father's company. Cora wasn't quite five feet tall and had an unusual combination of piercing blue eyes and red hair. She was generally quiet, and unless she was with people she was familiar with, she rarely started a conversation. Addison had been working with Cora on this issue for the last several years to bring her out of her shell. Cora was thirty-eight, single, and, Addison had recently discovered, wrote fan fiction. She never brought a plus one to a company event or had ever said anything about "we" when recalling what she'd done on vacation or over the weekend. The private lives of her staff weren't any of Addison's business, but she had a soft spot in her heart for Cora, and professionally, Cora had never let her down.

"I'm headed to an animal shelter called Haven. It's a full-cycle shelter in Jamaica."

"What's a full-cycle shelter?" Samantha Recker, the chief financial officer, who held the purse strings for what they were about to discuss, made a note on her iPad in front of her.

"They rescue dogs and cats and give them whatever medical

treatment they need, then find them new homes. There are thousands of them on the island." Cora held up her hands as if to stop a barrage of questions. "The founder is sometimes out for days trying to trap an animal. She'll stop anywhere and anytime she sees a stray. Once she was on her way to a wedding as the maid of honor, and she pulled over and rescued twelve puppies from a ditch. She was featured in their local magazine several months ago. For the really skittish animals, they have a halfway house to teach them how to be someone's pet."

"A halfway house?" Addison asked, taking off her reading glasses.

"Yeah. Some of these animals have been on their own for years, simply trying to survive. They're afraid of everything, especially people. Everyday noises that we take for granted, like the microwave beeping, or a shower running, or the toast popping up are a threat to them. The halfway house teaches them not to be afraid of the sounds found in a typical household. Once they're socialized, they're eligible to go to a good home. I'll be in the shelter or out in the field or wherever they need an extra hand. Our funding," she turned to Samantha, "thank you very much, will give them a new play yard, and we're planning to build more outdoor kennels."

Addison nodded. "Sounds like a great organization." She turned to Samantha.

"I was headed to the Maldives to set up a homeless shelter, but I was able to clear my schedule, so I'm leaving the day after tomorrow to go to the Bahamas, specifically Nassau," Samantha said. "I'm going to work with United Aid to help clean up after Hurricane Eduardo."

"That was an awful storm," Addison commented. "That was, what, a week ago? The destruction was awful."

Samantha nodded. "The people are proud and doing the best they can with little to no resources. Our funding will be a game changer." Samantha Recker lived up to her name, fancying fast motorcycles, hang gliding, and anything that caused her heart to race. Samantha was stunning and had somehow managed to evade being someone's wife. She stood almost six feet tall in her socks, and today she wore her long blond hair up in a French braid. Her manicured fingernail tapped the green folder in front of her.

"What about you, Boss?" Cora asked.

"Maui. I'm working with Habitat for Humanity. We're funding a women's build for three families."

"A women's build?"

"The work is done by women. Except for a few specialized contractors, every person on the build site is female. We're funding three houses this year," Addison said proudly. "I'm headed out on August first."

Cora jotted something down on her iPad. "I go July third."

Addison was proud of the way her team had embraced the volunteer program she'd started six years ago. She had inherited the company that previous year, when her father had dropped dead of a brain aneurysm on a job site. Addison had been twenty-nine, and even though she had spent almost fifteen years working beside her dad, she was still terrified.

Bradbury Construction had grown from a one-man handyman service to a small regional construction firm, and now it was one of the largest in the Southwest. From as far back as Addison could remember, they had never had quite enough to eat, their cramped, dilapidated house was either too hot or too cold, and the contents of the food box from the church supplemented the rice and beans and, on special occasions, the ground chuck that was on the dinner plate. Her clothes also came from the church donation box, and she wore her only pair of shoes for so long after they were too small that she almost caused permanent damage to her toes, all while her dad struggled to make his company successful. Addison remembered how sometimes her mother wouldn't eat, claiming she wasn't hungry when they all sat down around the dining-room table. Addison learned years later there wasn't enough to go around. One leg on the table was shorter than the other, and it was her job to make sure an old washcloth filled the gap during each meal. They might have been struggling, but their house was always filled with love and laughter.

When Addison assumed command of Bradbury, she had

instituted a policy of five paid volunteer days per year for every employee. Addison was a firm believer in giving back and would be forever grateful to those who had helped her and her family during the lean years.

When the financials of Bradbury shifted from being able to donate small cash contributions and volunteer days, she had proposed Let's Do This, the volunteer event they were talking about now.

She, Cora, and Samantha would spend four weeks volunteering their time with an agency of their choice. There were no rules other than it must be something where they as individuals, as well as funding from Bradbury, would make a significant difference. The other three members of her executive team had gone last year. Each of them had carried the program throughout their departments but certainly in not an extravagant manner.

Addison's team worked hard, and these two women specifically had worked their butts off the past eighteen months. Before Christmas, Addison had told them to choose an exotic location for their voluteerism, if at all possible. Even paradise had its needy. They'd be able to mix a little bit of relaxation along with their volunteer responsibilities.

Addison was looking forward to getting out from behind her desk and the stranglehold of her phone, paperwork, and meetings and back into the field. She missed the feel of a hammer in her hand and the smell of fresh-cut lumber. Building was her roots, ran through her blood, and was her livelihood.

"All right then," Addison said, closing her notebook. "Samantha, be careful out there. Let's get to work."

PART I

Bahama Breeze

Sam and Teresa

Chapter One

The destruction was everywhere. Even after almost a week, the damage caused by Eduardo, the strongest hurricane ever to hit the tiny island of Nassau, was overwhelming. It looked like it had happened yesterday. Sam's stomach churned as she peered out the window while she flew over the popular tourist destination. Some said it looked like a bomb had hit, and words were inadequate for others. Sam's heart was in her throat as she stared at the complete devastation of entire neighborhoods. Some appeared to have once been affluent, others no more than shanties.

Now it all looked the same—piles of debris. The resorts on the shoreline had suffered significant damage as well. Built by big money, they were designed to withstand torrential rain, gale-force winds, and storm surge. Many were still standing, however severely damaged. Trees were flattened to the ground or lay crisscrossed over each other or on top of buildings. As they approached the landing zone, they were close enough to the ground to see people cleaning up with brooms, rakes, and their bare hands.

"We'll be landing in five."

The pilot's voice crackled over her headset. She was in a Bell 125 helicopter, as all commercial flights to the island had been canceled. The airport had taken a direct blow, the tower a crumpled heap of brick, metal, and technology. The only flights in and out carried relief supplies and volunteers.

Five other passengers were strapped in, surveying the

destruction below. They wore the universal symbol of the Red Cross on the front and back of their white T-shirts and were coming to provide relief to the local emergency services that had been completely overwhelmed.

Their landing zone was a grocery-store parking lot that had been cleared for emergency vehicles. Another similar helicopter sat on the other end, parked perfectly between two white lines. Sam barely noticed a slight nudge as the helicopter settled on the black asphalt.

"Stay seated, folks. I'll let you know when it's safe to disembark."

Sam gathered her backpack, which contained only a few essentials. Her duffel bag had been weighed and stored in the rear of the aircraft. Sam had traveled all over the world on one adventure or another and had learned how to pack light.

The captain gave the all-clear, and Sam was the first to exit. The door opened, and a gust of hot, humid air hit her in the face and took her breath away. It was June in the Caribbean, where the humidity often exceeded the ambient temperature. Today was no different.

Sam carefully descended the three steps to the ground and pulled her sunglasses off the top of her head to provide some relief from the bright midday sun. Her fellow passengers chatted as they waited for their luggage to be pulled from the rear of the helicopter. From what Sam could tell from their conversation, this was not their first trip to a disaster zone.

Sam looked around and saw complete devastation in all directions. She had seen pictures on Facebook, the videos on the news, but it couldn't do justice to what she was seeing now.

Surrounding the perimeter of the parking lot was a mound of building debris consisting of metal, bricks, and a few other materials she couldn't identify from this distance. The actual grocery store was a pile of rubble, its roof no match for the one-hundred-and-eighty-mile-per-hour winds. A banner advertising blueberries for sale had somehow survived the winds and torrential rain and hung by a corner, billowing in the gentle, warm breeze.

"Here you go, miss," the pilot said, setting her duffel bag at her feet. "Are you expecting a ride?"

"Yes, I am. Someone should be here any moment." Her administrative assistant had arranged for a car to pick her up. She glanced at her old Timex Expedition. They had arrived fifteen minutes early.

"Thanks for the ride," she said, hefting her bag.

"You can wait inside," one of the aid workers said. "It's air conditioned, and you'll get enough heat and humidity."

"Thanks. I appreciate that," Sam replied and followed her fellow passengers inside a big white tent with a large red cross on the side.

"Good afternoon. How may I help you?" A petite blond woman sat behind a table, paperwork weighted down with assorted rocks scattered around in front of her.

"No, thank you. I don't need anything," Sam said. "I came in on the helicopter from Miami and my ride isn't here yet. One of your guys said it was okay to wait in here. It's much cooler."

"Absolutely. We have coffee over there." She pointed to a battered table under an industrial-sized coffee urn. "And juice and water in the fridge."

A cup of coffee would give her just the jolt of caffeine she needed, but she politely declined. She wasn't in a position to take from those who might really need it.

Sam watched as people came in and were directed to specific areas inside the tent. Everyone was greeted with a warm smile, offered a bottle of water, fruit, or a granola bar. She did her best to stay out of the way while keeping her eye on the entrance to the parking lot. Twenty-five minutes later a battered yellow car with the word TAXI on the dented passenger door stopped just outside the tent.

If the destruction she noticed from the air was bad, what she saw on the ground on the way to the United Aid offices was much worse. Broken and bent trees lay everywhere, their thick trunks snapped like toothpicks or twisted like licorice. Cars that had not been able to move safely under cover had been flipped upside down or lay on their side. One was perched on a roof, and several were in the middle of a flooded field. The cleanup in some areas was well under way. Trash and debris lined some streets, and other residents were still struggling for some sense of normalcy. It was apparent who had access to money and resources.

The driver introduced himself as Manny and kept apologizing for how long the trip was taking, his Bahamian accent so thick Sam had to concentrate to understand what he was saying. She had no idea where she was going and relied on her driver to get her to the aid station she'd been assigned. Several times they had to backtrack as a downed utility pole or tree still blocked the road.

Children played in the street, their laughter in direct contrast to the stunned expression on their parents' faces. What roofs remained were covered with blue tarps, the less fortunate with scraps of wood or sections of wooden fence.

"Here we are, ma'am."

Sam looked out the windshield as the driver pulled into a parking lot. Several battered trucks were parked haphazardly in a dirt lot across the street from a brown construction trailer. She handed the driver two twenties and grabbed her backpack and duffel from the seat beside her, then headed for the sign that said *United Aid Office*. She climbed the four rickety wooden steps and had to give the door a good tug to open it.

Sam had barely closed it behind her when a short, plump woman with an engaging smile greeted her.

"You must be Samantha Recker. We've been expecting you. You can set your bag over there. It'll be okay." The woman gestured to a spot by the door. "I'm Mildred Howard, but everyone calls me Mimi. We're so glad you could make it."

"Samantha Recker," she said out of habit, then felt completely ridiculous. "It was a little challenging to get here, but I'm glad I made it." Her assistant had somehow found her the last seat on the transport coming in today.

"Come. Sit down." Mimi pulled a chair over and brushed something off the seat. "I have all your paperwork here." Mimi tapped a blue folder in front of her with her finger. Her name was written in black ink on the tab. "I just need to see your passport, and then you can get started."

The door opened behind her, and Sam turned to see a tall, dark-haired woman stepping into the room. A jolt of interest mixed with something else coursed through her. Sam had an especially fine-tuned gaydar, and it was pinging on all cylinders.

"Geez, it's hot out there," the woman said, then stopped when she saw Sam. "I'm sorry, Mimi. I didn't know you had anyone in here."

Sam felt the heat from the woman's gray eyes as she looked her over. Her appraisal was bold and confident, the kind a woman has when she's used to getting what she goes after. A different place and a different time, and Sam would definitely let this woman catch her.

"It's okay, Teresa," Mimi said. "Samantha Recker, Teresa Tinsdale. Teresa is one of our full-time workers. You've been with us how long now, Teresa? Six or seven years?"

"Seven."

"Samantha's the woman I was telling you about, Teresa."

Teresa's eyes widened, and Sam wasn't sure if that was a good look or a bad one. The glint in her eyes a few moments later was the real deal. Sam stood and extended her hand.

"Pleased to meet you, Teresa."

Teresa stepped forward, and the moment their hands touched, a bolt of heat shot through Sam and settled in her stomach. Her entire focus shifted to only Teresa. Her dark hair was short, and the dark speckles in her eyes were big, the dimple in her left cheek a mirror to the one on the other side. The warmth of Teresa's palm increased Sam's body temperature several degrees, and something flared in Teresa's eyes.

"Likewise, Samantha. Mimi," Teresa said, her eyes not leaving Sam, "why don't you put her on my crew? I could use someone just like her."

Judging by the way Teresa was looking at her, the double entendre in her statement was no mistake. Sam was a thrill seeker but didn't mix business with pleasure. And she certainly wouldn't do anything to harm her company. She was, after all, on the company's dime. If she were volunteering on her own it would be a very different story, with Chapter One starting right now.

"That's a good idea. Your crew is short, with Donna and Rachel leaving this week." Mimi shuffled some papers on her desk and made a notation on one she pulled from a pile.

"Okay, Samantha. You're on the blue crew. Let me get your gear, and you'll be good to go."

Mimi stuck her pen in a cup with several others and walked toward the cabinet at the rear of the room.

"So, Samantha, where are you from?" Teresa asked, sitting on the edge of Mimi's desk, her long legs dangling in front of her.

"Phoenix, Arizona." Sam added the state, not sure where Teresa was from.

Teresa nodded. "I've never been there, but I hear it's hot."

"It can be." Again, Sam read another double meaning in her words. Or was it just wishful thinking on her part? Geez. She'd been on the island less than an hour, and the heat coursing through her had nothing to do with the weather. "But that's only a few months out of the year. The rest is beautiful. What about you? Your accent sounds like you're from the Northeast."

"Connecticut."

"How did you come to be working here?" Sam asked, noticing that Mimi was sidelined in a conversation with another aid worker.

"Something to do," Teresa said offhandedly.

"This is quite a commitment for something to do."

"I like keeping busy."

Obviously, Sam wasn't going to get any additional information, so she switched tactics.

"So, what will we be working on? Tell me about the blue team."

"There are eight of us—four men, and with you now, three women plus me. We're assigned a specific area of the island, and our job is to clean up the debris left over from this shitstorm Eduardo. Just like a man to leave all his crap behind." Teresa smirked and winked. Sam's pulse kicked up.

"Anyway, we cut down trees and tear down anything that's not safe. We have a couple of trackhoes, and we push all of it to the street. We do general cleanup and whatever we can to help the homeowner or the business. Right now, Royale and Dominique are working on reopening a small mom-and-pop general store. François, Daniel, Martin, and Ray are shoring up a roof that wants to collapse on a house full of kids. Do you know how to operate a chainsaw?"

"Yes. I'm probably a little rusty, but I can also run a trackhoe, a bobcat, and a backhoe."

Teresa's eyebrows rose. "Excellent. We can definitely use you. The others are good but don't have any heavy-equipment experience. You look like you can handle yourself in just about any situation," Teresa commented, again glancing over her, her eyes lingering a little too long on her lips.

Sam didn't know if she should be flattered by Teresa's attention or if it was inappropriate.

"Okay, Sam. Here's your equipment," Mimi said, drawing Sam out of her thoughts.

Mimi handed her a blue safety vest with reflective tape, a blue hard hat, and a pair of black-and-yellow work gloves. "I'm sorry it took me so long. I got sidetracked. Teresa will show you everything you need to know."

"You bet I will, Mimi. Come on, Samantha. I'll show you where to store your gear."

CHAPTER TWO

D o you go by Samantha or Sam?" Teresa hoped it was Sam. The woman walking beside her did not look like a Samantha.

"Samantha is my work name. I prefer Sam."

It surprised Teresa how much she enjoyed saying Sam's name. "Okay. Sam it is."

Mimi had spoken about their new volunteer several times, and she had expected another frumpy, Earth-saving woman with not enough sense to pour pee out of a boot. She'd been more than a little surprised when Mimi introduced her. Sam was a few inches taller than her own five foot ten inches, and her long blond hair was up in a French braid. Her eyes were an unusual shade of deep emerald green. In addition, her handshake was firm, not the limp, barely there grip of most women and, even worse, some men.

"What brings you here?"

"Probably the same reason everyone else comes, to help. I have a few skills and some time, so here I am."

"Mimi said you're staying for a month. That's a lot of time. What do you do when you're not volunteering?"

"I'm the chief financial officer of a construction firm."

"Brains and skills, a fine combination." And one Teresa found very sexy. She took Sam's elbow and steered her away from a muddy pothole. The burn that traveled through her was just as powerful as when they shook hands.

"And you get a month off?" Teresa liked hearing Sam talk, her voice like a cool balm on this hot summer day.

"My boss is big on giving back. We each pick where we want to go, and we rotate. This is my year."

"And you chose here."

"Actually, no," Sam said. "I was headed for the Maldives, but when I heard about the hurricane and saw the destruction, I just had to come. I've always loved the islands, and I wanted to do something to help."

"Well, I'm glad you're here. This is where we bunk." Teresa stopped in front of a blue-and-white trailer larger than a camping trailer but smaller than a mobile home. "We have a generator that gives us power for the lights and the water pump. The men are over there." She pointed to a green-and-white trailer that was the mirror image of the one they were standing in front of. Teresa pulled a key ring from her pocket, handed her a key, and unlocked and opened the door. She motioned for Sam to go ahead and enjoyed the view of Sam's backside as she went up the three steps to go inside.

The interior consisted of five beds—two in the rear and three in front. The beds were larger than a cot but smaller than a twin bed. A small refrigerator, a two-burner stove, a microwave on a counter above a few cabinets served as a kitchen, and two chairs and a small love seat separated the sleeping areas.

"The shower and toilet are in here." Teresa opened a narrow door. "Not much hot water, so make it quick. United provides breakfast and dinner in the chow trailer, and they make us a lunch to take with us. The open bunks are that one in the back," she pointed to a bed next to hers, "and this one here by the door. If I were you, I'd take that one." Teresa pointed toward the bed next to hers. "Less coming and going."

Teresa could almost hear Sam weigh the pros and cons of each in her head.

"I'll take the back one."

"You and your gear are safe here. Just us girls have a key. Royale and Dominique are good people. Actually, they're nuns. We dropped the sister."

"Can't get safer than that, I suppose," Sam replied, smiling and pointing to the heavens.

Teresa's heart skipped when Sam smiled at her own comment. Even in jeans and work boots, she was breathtaking, and Teresa had to blink a few times to regain her equilibrium.

"Do I need anything else?" Sam asked, holding her hard hat and gloves. Teresa hadn't noticed when she had put on her vest.

"No. You're good. Let's go."

Sam asked intelligent questions about the work they were doing as Teresa drove them to the area they were currently focusing on. She inquired about the local emergency relief and how the residents were doing. Teresa was impressed that Sam understood the magnitude of the job in front of them.

"We're working in this area," Teresa said as they passed the piles of red bricks and corrugated tin scattered everywhere. "It's a four-block area that used to be a neighborhood of mostly resort workers. Today's our first day here." Teresa stopped and pulled the key out of the ignition.

"Looks like we walk from here." Sam followed and stood beside her as they surveyed the site.

"Jesus," Sam murmured.

"My words exactly. The storm practically obliterated everything in his path, and the islands took a direct hit. Mother Nature was pretty pissed," Teresa added.

Teresa had spent most of the last seven years in places just like this. She'd seen the aftermath of earthquakes that left nothing but rubble, the survivors bloodied and broken and others not so lucky when pulled from the rubble. She had mopped up after wildfires had ravaged neighborhoods and searched for bodies in the receding waters of a tsunami.

She was thirty-three and had seen more destruction, both natural and manmade, than she ever thought possible. Oddly she felt more at peace than she'd ever been.

Teresa had been born into money—big, big money—the only child of parents who had no qualms about taking every advantage of it and using it to influence others to get what they wanted. When her parents married, they had combined their inheritance into even bigger money. They never held a job in their lives and socialized with others equally as fortunate. They had no idea what it was like to work for something or even want anything. It was either handed to them on the proverbial silver platter—or, in their case, gold—or they just bought it.

Teresa had the best nannies money could buy and went to the best schools the world had to offer. She played with the children of kings, sheiks, and some of the richest people in the world. The only expectation of her was to not embarrass her parents and to uphold her family's place in the top one percent. Teresa filled that role perfectly until the incident that changed her life.

She had been walking down a bustling street in Europe with some equally self-centered friends, when she saw three girls who couldn't have been more than six or seven years old skipping toward them from the other direction. Their clothes were worn and tattered, the shoes on their feet almost nonexistent. Teresa wasn't sure exactly what happened, but the next thing she knew, brakes were squealing, people were screaming, and blood was everywhere. Somehow two of the girls had ended up underneath a delivery truck, and the other lay crumpled on the side of the road at her feet. She was horrified by the scene and dropped to her knees next to the little girl.

"Don't touch her!" one of her friends shouted. "Everything's bloody. You'll catch something."

Teresa ignored her and took the girl's hand. She knew enough not to try to move her, but she could offer some comfort. The girl's eyes fluttered open.

"You're going to be okay," Teresa said, staring into frightened dark eyes. "Emergency services are on the way." Teresa doubted the girl spoke English, but she seemed to understand her soft tone. "I'm Teresa," she said, patting herself on the chest to indicate that was her name.

The girl tried to speak, but only a moan came out.

"It's okay. Just lie still. You're going to be okay," she repeated, brushing her hair out of her bloody face.

"Teresa, what are you doing? Let's go. We don't want to get involved in this," one of her friends said, her displeasure apparent.

"Yeah, T. She's just a street urchin," the other one said, sounding equally disgusted.

"Shut up," Teresa barked. "Can't you see she's just a little girl? She's hurt and scared. Where is your compassion? Just go. I'll meet you back at the hotel." Teresa wasn't surprised when they did just that without protest.

Teresa stayed with the girl, holding her hand and talking to her until the ambulance arrived. The little girl's eyes never left Teresa's. When the medics nudged Teresa out of the way, she let go of her hand and the girl cried out. They let Teresa take her hand again until she was loaded into the ambulance. The medics spoke English and had told Teresa the little girl's name was Nadia.

When Teresa got back to the hotel, her friends were waiting for her. She knew she couldn't tolerate any comments they would make about her actions, so she went directly to her room, collapsed on the bed, and sobbed.

Unbeknownst to anyone, Teresa had tracked down where Nadia had been taken and paid her medical bills. She also anonymously paid for the funeral of the other two girls.

Her parents were involved in all the right charities and attended the requisite benefits and auctions and had written off millions of dollars in tax-deductible donations. But it was no more than lip service, and Teresa had been following in her parents' footsteps until that day. She did her research and created a foundation to provide care and services for children whose parents couldn't afford it. Her parents, of course, had no idea.

Previously, if she were in this situation, where everything she had had been destroyed, she'd just charter a helicopter, check into some high-end hotel, buy everything she needed, and have it delivered and set up the next day. Now her work filled her with purpose, and it meant something to help others not as fortunate as she was.

Teresa never showed vulnerability, never showed how much this work meant to her. Her parents didn't know the direction her life had taken. They thought she was just jetting around the world. She visited them twice a year and lied her way through a week's obligatory visit. They didn't even care enough to inquire any deeper. Daughterly duties performed, Teresa would go back and immerse herself in her aid work every day before the sun came up until long after the sun went down, until she collapsed in exhaustion.

❖

"Can you handle her?" Teresa asked, pointing to the smaller of two trackhoes parked on the street. The machines were CAT backhoes, the front bucket modified with a grabbing mechanism that opened and closed like a claw to pick up and move large amounts of debris.

Sam carefully walked around the rig, opened the door of the cab, and climbed up inside. The cab was small, and she situated her long legs as best she could. The controls were slightly different than what she was used to; however, they were basically the same—they raised and lowered the bucket and opened and closed the claw. Her hands looked naked with her short nails and no jewelry. She jumped down from the cab.

"Yes. I can handle her. Where do you want me to start?"

Teresa looked at her watch. "Let's have lunch first. Everyone's on the next block, and I'll introduce you around."

Teresa introduced everyone, explaining who was who. Daniel was a pastor of a church in Idaho, and Martin and Francis were brothers from Brussels and had arrived two days earlier. They spoke perfect English and had Sam laughing at the stories of their adventures across Europe. Sisters Royale and Dominique were from a Catholic church in New Jersey and had the solid handshakes and accent to go with their hometown. Ray was from Bolivia and had worked with United Aid for four years. Teresa was evasive and just said she was from Connecticut.

They dug into their lunch, and the blue crew sat on their equipment or, like Sam and Teresa, the ground as their makeshift lunch table. In between bites, Ray gave her a general overview of

United Aid's work in the country and what they had been working on for the past week.

Sam had chosen United Aid because of their record of humanitarian work around the world and their stellar reputation in the disaster-relief community. Far too often the majority of donations provided to agencies were, in fact, paid to staff and used for administrative fees, with a small percentage buying the actual supplies. Those who had a solid roof over their heads, food in their pantry, and clean water running out of their taps lined their pockets when those less fortunate had lost everything except what they could carry. Sam did an extensive amount of research before signing up and signing the company check.

"So, Sam, tell us about yourself?" Martin asked, wiping his hands on a paper napkin.

"I live in Phoenix, Arizona. That's one of the states in the US," she added for the others. Then she gave them the CliffsNotes version of her job and why she'd come.

"Are you married or have any children?" Dominique asked.

She felt Teresa's eyes on her.

"No to both."

Dominique asked a follow-up question. "Are you a career woman?"

Teresa stifled a chuckle. "Don't be offended. She asks everyone that question."

"No problem. I do believe you can have both, but I haven't met anyone I want to spend the rest of my life with." She looked at Teresa, and her pulse kicked up while her stomach flip-flopped. Something flickered in Teresa's eyes, and she quickly glanced away.

"Are you a lesbian?" Melba, the local woman whose house they were currently working on, asked. Teresa choked on her sandwich.

"Miss Melba, you don't ask somebody that," Daniel said.

"Why not?"

"Because it's none of your business. And because if she's not, then you either made her angry or embarrassed her. And she might not want to even tell you if she was."

"That's okay, Melba." Sam swung her eyes over to Teresa, then back to Melba. "Yes, I am. Does that make a difference?" If Teresa hadn't figured it out before, she certainly knew now.

"Not to me," Melba replied.

"You Americans are so hung up on sex," Martin commented and shook his head.

Daniel spoke up. "Well, I don't speak for all Americans, but I have no problem with sex." Everybody looked at him. "What? I'm a pastor, not a priest. Just ask my wife." They all laughed.

"Okay. Let's get back to work." Teresa stood, and everyone rose to their feet, ready to finish the day.

❖

Sam was good. After getting used to the controls, she handled the machine like she drove it every day. She was efficient and careful, making sure the debris she was moving was handled safely with minimal impact on the area around her. Teresa had had several men on her crew who simply dragged it to a pile, not caring about the damage they left behind. Sam seemed to understand that even though this was now nothing but debris, it had once been someone's home—where they raised their kids, laughed around the dinner table, and made love in a warm, dry bed. Once-treasured material things were now broken pieces of their lives. Teresa was glad Sam was on her crew.

Chainsaws buzzed all day, accompanied by the annoying beep, beep, beep of the reverse gear on the trackhoe. The safety feature on the machine was ear-splitting. Teresa kept an eye on Sam, and she worked nonstop. Unlike so many others she'd had to give step-by-step instructions to, Sam instinctively knew what to do.

People were returning to what was left of their homes, undergoing a combination of shock and despair and occasionally relief. One woman who realized her house was nothing but rubble fell to her knees and wept.

Sam turned off the machine and let her grieve in silence. After several moments Sam climbed out of the cab, brushed off her clothes, removed her hard hat, and approached the woman. She knelt next to her.

Teresa couldn't hear what was said between the two of them but watched as the woman turned to Sam and threw herself into her arms and sobbed. Sam held her for at least five minutes, then helped her to her feet. The woman leaned on Sam as they approached the ruins of her life.

"That was a wonderful thing you did for her," Teresa said, motioning toward the place the woman had once called home. They had taken a break, each of them pulling a wet cloth out of the cooler. They combated the heat and humidity by filling an ice chest with ice and cold water and immersing towels they would then pull out and drape over their heads and wrap around their necks.

"I can't imagine what she must be going through." Sam looked at her, anguish and strength in her eyes. "Does it get any easier?" she asked.

Teresa didn't need Sam to explain what the *it* was. "If it does, then it's time to quit and do something else."

Teresa knew Sam's company, Bradbury Construction, had donated a huge amount of money to the relief effort. Mimi had let it slip one day and had sworn Teresa to secrecy. The caliber of Bradbury employees was evident in Samantha Recker.

"What did you say to her?"

Sam thought for a moment and frowned. "I don't remember. But it seemed to have helped. A good cry doesn't hurt either."

Teresa turned at a noise behind her. It was the woman, and she held something in her hands, handing it to Sam.

"This is for you, miss. It is to keep you safe."

It was a necklace made of leather and beaded in the middle— beautiful and obviously homemade.

Sam hurried to her feet. "Thanks are not necessary, Consuelo. I can't take this. It is yours, and surely very special to you."

"Please. It is my way of honoring you for your assistance to my community."

Teresa tried to get Sam's attention to somehow signal her that it would be rude not to accept such a gift, but it turned out she didn't need to.

Sam reverently took the necklace in both hands and held it as if it were the most precious of gifts.

"Thank you, Consuela. I will cherish it forever. Would you?" Sam indicated for Consuela to tie the necklace behind her neck.

Consuela's hands were scraped and dirty, and after Sam moved her hair away, she tied the cord. Sam turned back around, her fingers on the beads, and then took Consuela's hand in hers. "Thank you again. I am honored. Be safe."

They sat in silence for several more minutes, and then Sam quietly went back to work.

CHAPTER THREE

S am sat next to Royale, a petite, dark-haired woman who hadn't said much during lunch, and dinner seemed to be more of the same. "Do you volunteer with United Aid often?"

"Our parish does, but this is my first time."

"Quite a big one to cut your teeth on."

Royale simply nodded, her eyes not meeting Sam's.

"I'm not Catholic and don't mean to be rude, but how long have you been at your parish?" Sam was an awful judge of age, but Royale looked to be in her late twenties.

"Four years."

"Are you from New Jersey originally?"

"Yes."

Obviously, an extended conversation with Royale was out of the question, at least for right now. Sam asked a few more questions to be polite, but Royale wasn't the talkative type. Dominique, on the other hand, chatted away about anything and everything and didn't mince words.

"May I have your attention, please," Mimi called, clapping her hands to get everyone's attention.

Mimi relayed a few announcements, pointing out the new people who had arrived, where they came from, and how long they would be on the island. Even though she was good with names, no way could Sam remember forty-two people, at least not in the first few days. The volunteers included a variety of shapes, sizes, gender, and nationality. She was proud to be with them.

The teams sat together, except for a few who were intermixed with others. Teresa sat down across from her, her plate filled with two hamburgers, potato chips, and three large pickles. It was clear that Teresa had the respect of not only her crew, but others as well, though she didn't seem to be aware of it. She didn't dominate the conversation or draw attention to herself. Several other team leaders had come by and asked her opinion about something or advice on how to get something done.

"What's new on the admin front?" Ray asked.

"The admin front?" Sam asked.

"Teresa is the team lead, and she has to go to all the administrative meetings and take care of all the paperwork," Dominique said.

"I'd rather be shoveling debris than paperwork, but we all have our cross to bear." Teresa blushed and looked at Dominique and Royale. "Excuse me, Sisters. No offense."

"None taken," Dominique replied easily. "We all have crap to do in our jobs."

Sam choked on a chip that got caught in her throat.

"Are you okay?" Ray asked, slapping her on the back a few times.

"Yes. Just caught by surprise that Dominique has crap in her job."

"Honey, there's crap in every job on this earth. Jesus himself had more than his share."

Everyone on the blue team agreed.

Sam really liked Dominique. She had never met a nun, and Dominique certainly was not what she'd expected. But of course, her view of nuns was shaped by the movies and television. How wrong was that?

"Well?" Dominique asked Teresa, waiting for an answer to her original question.

"Nothing much. We're good to stay in our area, and they target us to be done in about six days."

"Six days," Daniel said, obviously incredulous. "Do they think we can work miracles?" He sheepishly looked at Dominique and Royale. "Sorry."

"With Sam on our crew and the way she handles the trackhoe, we'll get it done," Teresa replied confidently.

"You're pretty good on that thing," Dominique said. They had arrived where Teresa and Sam had been working earlier that afternoon. "Better than you, Daniel."

"Anyone's better than me," he said.

"You take care of the people's homes," Royale said, surprising Sam.

"It's just that, their homes. I know if my possessions had been destroyed, I wouldn't want them treated like trash. To us it is, but not to them. They've already lost so much, they don't need that kind of insult piled on top of it."

She felt Teresa's eyes on her from across the table. Sam met them, and she saw respect in her gaze.

"So, what do you do when you're not cleaning up after a disaster?" she asked Teresa.

Teresa's eyes masked something Sam couldn't identify. "A little of this and a little of that," she answered evasively.

"And what little is that exactly?" Sam asked.

"Does it matter?" Teresa asked in a joking tone, but Sam saw right through her reaction. Teresa didn't like people pressing for more specifics.

"Unless this is your atonement for some grievous sin, some horrid behavior, or you're running from the law, no, it doesn't."

Dominique snickered.

"And if I had committed some grievous sin, had behaved horridly, or was running from the law?"

"It's not up to me why you're here. But from what I've seen so far, and what others have said, this is where you want to be."

"I wouldn't listen to gossip, but in this case it's true. This is exactly where I want to be."

"Me too. I'm just here to help in any way."

"That's a coincidence. That's my job too. In addition to the paperwork," she added.

"Tell us about your family, Sam," Daniel asked.

"My parents live in Albuquerque, New Mexico. My dad is a pharmacist and my mom a teacher. They have three kids other than me, and seven grandkids scattered around the country."

"How long are you here for?"

"A month."

"I wish I could stay that long," Daniel said wistfully. "These people need so much."

"That's why we're here, Daniel, to help in any way that we can. The work you all," Teresa nodded to the others, "are doing will help give some sense of normalcy to the neighborhood."

"We should be done the day after tomorrow at the latest," Ray added.

Silence ensued for the next several minutes as they finished their dinner. Some got up to get coffee, and Sam declined when Ray offered to get her a cup.

She stifled a yawn. "I think I'll turn in," she said. "I'm used to sitting behind a desk all day, and I'm beat."

"I'll walk you back." Teresa stood.

"That's not necessary," Sam said.

"Probably not, but it's still your first day, so you're my responsibility. Tomorrow you're on your own."

Sam knew that was just a figure of speech. So far, it was apparent that Teresa looked after her entire crew.

"You don't like to talk about yourself," Sam commented as they walked back to the bunkhouse. The sun had set, and she slapped a mosquito that landed on her arm.

"None of this is about me," Teresa replied. "And besides, I'm not real interesting."

"Everyone is interesting," Sam said.

"Sorry to disappoint, but I'm not," Teresa said, clearly ending the conversation by unlocking and opening the door to their sleeping quarters.

"You can shower first," Teresa said as the door was closing behind them. "But…"

"Make it fast." Sam echoed Teresa's earlier words.

"Glad to see you pay attention."

"I am very observant and pay very close attention," Samantha said, her pulse skittering as she looked Teresa in the eye. Two could play at the double-entendre game.

Sam gathered her toiletries and PJs and stepped into the small but efficient bathroom. The shower was pocket-sized but roomy enough to get the job done without banging her elbows on the wall too many times. She was in and out in less than five minutes, using another five to brush her teeth and get dressed.

Teresa was sitting in one of the chairs, her legs propped up on a stool. Her head was back and her eyes closed. Sam took the opportunity to look at her unchecked.

Teresa was beautiful in an unpretentious, earthy sort of way. Her skin was tan from hours in the sun, and the lines around her eyes when she smiled were now smooth. Her hands looked strong, and Sam could see the muscles in her forearms were from physical labor, not the gym. She suspected the rest of her body was equally toned. But it was what Sam had felt when she first saw her that she couldn't get out of her mind.

Sam was, by profession, methodical in calculating where all the pieces needed to fit together. In her world two plus two always equaled a definitive four. She was a risk taker, but a calculated one. She weighed the options of the unknown, then made a fact-based decision. She wasn't ruled by her gut, but she did have an innate ability to see what the end looked like. She was usually a great judge of character and of people and was rarely wrong. She chose her women with the same thoughtful approach. Some were more adventurous, several more turned into good friends, and only one, surprisingly, was a nightmare. She wasn't sure where Teresa fit into that equation and frowned as she thought about that uncertainty. Sam brought herself back to reality with a jolt. Why was she even thinking of Teresa in either category?

"Have you decided?"

Teresa's voice startled her. She'd been trying so hard to wrap her head around where Teresa fit that she hadn't noticed Teresa's eyes were on her.

"On what?" she managed to say.

"On whatever put that concentrating look on your face. You look like you were trying to decide on something."

Sam said the first thing that came to mind. "Just if I wanted to take some ibuprofen before I went to bed or in the morning. I know I'm going to feel it."

Teresa looked at her as if trying to decide if she was telling the truth. Finally, she said, "Probably both. It'll help you sleep better and give you a jump-start on sore muscles tomorrow. There's cold water in the fridge."

"You're probably right. Thanks."

Teresa got out of the chair and could feel the heat from Sam's body as she walked by her. She detected the scent of jasmine, which she remembered from this morning.

She hadn't been sleeping when Sam exited the bathroom. She was imagining her naked in the shower, water sliding down her skin. It was all she could do not to put her hand down her pants and expand on the vision in her head. She'd have to save that for another, more private time. Who was she kidding? There was no privacy, evident by Royale and Dominique entering the bunkhouse as she was gathering her bathroom gear.

"I'll just be a few minutes, ladies," Teresa said, closing the door behind her.

As the water ran, Teresa decided this was about as private as she was going to get, so she closed her eyes and slid her hand between her legs.

"How was your first day?" Teresa asked, climbing into her bed. Sam was lying on her side facing her.

"Exhausting, but great. I'm going to be sore in places I don't even know I have."

"How did you learn to drive?" Teresa asked, referencing her ability to handle the big machines.

"I grew up around it. My best friend Addison, her father owned the company I work for. I spent summers working on one of his construction crews. I'm out of practice, and obviously technology has changed, but it's still basically the same."

"Will my light bother you?" Teresa asked, sliding under the covers. A small reading light above her head was on. She liked to read before she fell asleep. Stories of other worlds calmed her racing thoughts. Tonight, they were definitely on full speed. Her moment in the shower had been just that—a moment. She needed much more than that.

"No, not at all," Sam replied. "Why do *you* do this?"

Sam's question surprised her. "Because I want to, and I can." Teresa hoped her flippant answer would do, but something told her that Sam wouldn't stop asking until she got a satisfactory answer.

"Surely you don't go from one disaster to another? Do they even happen like that?"

"Yes. You'd be surprised what happens around the world that the US news doesn't report."

"Is there someplace you call home?"

"Not really. I have a place in Connecticut, but I'm not there much," Teresa replied honestly. When others had asked, she had never gone into even this little bit of detail.

"Are you sure you're not running from the law?"

Teresa was running from a lot of things, but the law wasn't one of them.

"Positive. You'd better get some sleep. Breakfast is at seven thirty."

Sam had captured Teresa's attention the moment she saw her sitting at Mimi's desk. Attractive women always caught her eye, but there was something more to Sam than just her dazzling smile and knockout body. Teresa didn't understand how she knew that after only one day. At first it was just the typical zing of attraction, but even then, it felt different. She couldn't put her finger on it, but she'd figure it out. She always did.

Teresa opened her book and tried to read, but her attention was on the woman sleeping beside her. Well, not beside her, beside her. Sam was about five feet away against the other wall. Dominique and Royale had come in earlier and were on their knees quietly saying their evening devotions, their heads bowed.

Chapter Four

S am woke to the scent of coffee. She opened her eyes when the sound of a cup hitting the table brought the delicious scent even closer. A pair of legs covered in worn jeans was in front of her. Samantha ran her eyes up past lean hips, the enticing swell of breasts, the curve of the tanned neck, past smiling lips, and landed on crystal-clear dark eyes.

"Good morning. I thought you could use this," Teresa said, pointing to the cup. "The first morning after is always tough." The twinkling in Teresa's eyes was just not fair, Samantha thought. Teresa was up dressed, put together, and more than likely had brushed her teeth. Sam, on the other hand, was in wrinkled boxers and a bunched-up T-shirt, her hair a mess, and her breath probably smelling like something she didn't want to think about.

"Thanks," Sam croaked. Great. She had a frog voice and needed to pee. The only other thing that would make her morning perfect would be if she had started her period. She sat up and stuffed her pillow behind her.

"What time is it? Did I oversleep?" Sam looked around for her phone. Teresa picked it up off the floor and handed it to her. It must've fallen off the table beside the bed.

"No. It's only seven, but I'm an early riser. That, and I have a team meeting every morning." Teresa chuckled.

Teresa gestured toward the cup. "I didn't know how you took it."

"Thanks. I take it black. I was never awake enough to put anything in it." Sam brought the cup to her lips and inhaled. "The only thing better than the first cup of the day is when someone else brings to you."

"Does that happen often? Someone bringing you coffee in the morning," Teresa asked, sitting down on her bed facing Sam.

Sam fought not to choke on her first sip. She slowly took another swallow before answering.

"I don't kiss and tell." Sam's voice was husky, but this time not from sleep.

"Good to know."

Teresa's eyes burned into Sam's so intently her body was suddenly on alert, including her nipples in her braless state.

"Good morning, ladies." Dominique spoke from her side of the room. "It's another blessed day."

"Yes, it is," Teresa said, breaking her paralyzing eye contact. "And we better get to breakfast before the yellow team does. They ate all the bacon yesterday."

Sam felt Teresa's eyes on her as she gathered her things and her coffee and slipped into the bathroom. She exhaled deeply when she closed the door. It was only a thin layer of hollow wood, but judging by the way she had reacted to Teresa this morning, she needed every piece of defense she could get.

She finished quickly, washing her face and brushing her teeth longer than usual. She hadn't brought her clothes in with her, the room too small for anything other than donning sleepwear.

Royale and Dominique were making their beds while Teresa sat in the chair, a pile of paperwork in her lap. Sam took a pair of jeans from the shelf, and after kicking off her boxers, she stepped into her briefs, then her jeans. Her back was to the women when she repeated similar actions, finally pulling her T-shirt over her head. She felt Teresa's eyes on her the entire time and hoped her face wasn't as flushed as the rest of her felt. When she turned around to put on her boots, she risked a glance at Teresa. Her head was down, her eyes on the papers, but Sam saw her hand shake when she turned a page.

"Did you sleep well? I sleep better here than at home. Must be all the physical labor. It's good for you," Dominique said before she opened the bathroom door.

"Yes, I did. Thanks."

"You two go ahead. Royale and I have to say our morning devotions," Dominique said.

"There's more coffee," Teresa said as Sam laced her boots. "I'm no expert, but it's better than what they serve in the chow hall. I guess it's hard to make gallons of it taste good."

Sam looked at Teresa as she poured another cup. Teresa had dark circles under her eyes, the indication of a restless night.

"Something wrong?" Teresa asked.

"What? Oh, no. Sorry." Sam stumbled through her words, having been caught staring.

"We should head over for breakfast. I like to give the sisters some privacy to get ready."

How thoughtful, Sam mused. She had no problem sharing space with other women. She was used to it from her days playing high school and college basketball. She assumed nuns were a little more private.

"Sounds good. I'm ready."

They were silent as they traversed the camp compound. Several others were milling about or heading to breakfast as well.

"It's going to be hot today," Teresa said, looking up into the cloudless sky.

"I'm used to the heat but not this humidity," Sam said. "In Phoenix, the temperature often exceeds one hundred ten, but the humidity is always in the single digits."

"Push the fluids and find shade as often as you can," Teresa said.

It was what they'd done yesterday. Sam was surprised her pee wasn't red from all the cherry Gatorade she'd consumed.

"I thought I was going to float away yesterday. But the more I drank, the more I sweated."

"That's the secret. It's when you stop sweating that you get into trouble. Do your hands hurt?"

"Excuse me?"

"Do your hands hurt? Most people's hands hurt from gripping a shovel or a rake or the controls on one of the machines."

Sam opened and closed her hands a few times. "No. Surprisingly I don't feel too bad." She was amazed that she didn't ache all over. Her knees were a little stiff, but that was a remnant of running up and down the basketball court for over twenty years.

"Good, because we have another full day."

The next several days were copies of the day before. A hearty breakfast was followed by cutting, hauling, and the backbreaking work of restoring neighborhoods to something that didn't resemble a war zone.

The residents welcomed them with open arms, greeting them with hugs and tears of joy. This was a completely different world for Sam. She had never experienced any level of destruction, especially the aftereffects these wonderful people were facing every day. Their spirit was intact, even though their homes and livelihood lay shattered around them.

She saw neighbors cooking together, sharing what little they had. An extension cord plugged into a communal generator snaked through rubble to power a noisy portable air conditioner in a house that was relatively intact. On one street, dozens of residents were cleaning up the yard of one house before moving on to the next. Neighbor helping neighbor was clearly evident. Why couldn't people treat each other like this every day?

It was the evenings that were different. The teams still had the same camaraderie and challenges, and they would sit around the campfire, where someone would bring out a guitar and another a contraband bottle of booze.

Teresa always waited until Sam had sat down, and then she somehow managed to find an empty spot facing her. Everyone would talk for a few hours until they drifted off to another part of the camp or went back to their bunkhouse.

"I'm turning in," Dominique said, one evening after Sam had been there a week. "Walk with me, Sam?"

Sam wanted to stay right where she was, caught in the fire of

Teresa's eyes. Unfortunately, Dominique stepped between them, breaking the spell.

"Sure." She needed to catch her breath.

Teresa didn't hide the disappointment in her eyes.

"What do you think so far?" Dominique asked. She put her arm through Sam's for extra balance. She was in her mid-sixties, after all.

"I know I made the right choice coming here. There's so much need, and the people are wonderful. It's been a little less than two weeks, but I'm tempted to give up my job and do this forever."

"Then you'd be just like Teresa."

"That would be interesting, wouldn't it?"

"I think she's running from something," Dominique said confidently.

Sam was surprised. "You do?"

"I may be old, but I have a direct link to the big guy upstairs. And he sees everything," she said by way of explanation.

"And he passes that information on to you?"

"Absolutely. That and the fact that after forty-five years in the Church, I know when someone is running."

"Like running from the authorities?" Sam asked.

"No. Her own inner demons. Something is troubling that girl."

"And you're telling me this because?" Sam let the last word draw out.

"Because I see the way she looks at you."

Again, Sam was surprised at the comment and the observation behind it. She'd thought no one was paying any attention. Boy, was she wrong if a nun picked up on the electricity between them.

"That's just biology," Sam explained.

"That's a big part of it, but I think you can help her stop running and forgive herself."

Dominique's conversation ran through Sam's mind as she got ready for bed. She tried to stay awake until Teresa came in, but her eyes closed, and she drifted off.

Sam woke, every muscle aching. She lay on her back listening to the sounds of the night. The hum of portable generators displaced the normal chirping of crickets in the night air. Dominique and Royale were sleeping quietly on the other side of the room. She got up to use the bathroom and was pulling up the covers when Teresa moaned. When she did it again, Sam sat up and looked at her. At first, she thought Teresa was having a sex dream, her arms and legs moving restlessly. Sam was suddenly hot all over. Who was she dreaming about? What were they doing? Who was doing who? Sam's clit started throbbing. She glanced at Dominique and Royale, worried that they would hear Teresa. God. How embarrassing would that be?

"No."

Sam's attention went back to Teresa. What had she said?

"No. Please don't move."

What the fuck? This was not a sex dream. Teresa's tone and body movements had changed.

"You're going to be okay. I'm here with you."

Sam didn't know if she should wake Teresa or just let her be. She was obviously in distress. She probably wouldn't even remember the dream in the morning. She swung her feet to the floor, the tile cool.

"She's had them before."

Royale's voice pierced the darkness.

"What?"

"Teresa. She's had the same nightmare several times."

"Should I wake her?"

"If we hear her, we do. She goes right back to sleep. We don't think she even remembers in the morning because she's never said anything to us." Light from the moon filtered through a space in the curtain. Teresa's face was contorted in pain, and Sam ran her fingers across her forehead. Her skin was hot and clammy. Sam thought she calmed a little as she stroked her face.

"Shh," Sam whispered when Teresa moaned again. "Shh. You're all right. It's just a bad dream." Sam kept her voice soothing, and Teresa turned her face into Sam's palm when she covered her cheek. "It's okay. You're going to be okay." Sam kept repeating the same words until Teresa quieted her restless movements. Sam didn't return to her bed until she was certain Teresa was in a dreamless sleep.

The next morning Teresa was up and out when Sam woke. If not for the nightmare and the rumpled bedding, Sam would've thought Teresa hadn't come back. A jolt of jealousy shot through her as she imagined another woman's hands on Teresa.

"That's ridiculous," Samantha said, tossing off the covers and heading toward the bathroom.

CHAPTER FIVE

Y ou said you know how to use a chainsaw."

"Yes. Like everything else, it's been a while."

"Good, because we need to clear the next street first."

Teresa dropped the men off, and then she and Sam proceeded to their assignment for the day. Dominique and Royale had the day off, and Sam rode shotgun. Teresa parked and opened the rear cargo area of the van. She pointed to one of the smaller chainsaws.

"Why don't you start with that one." She pointed to the yellow one. "It's a little easier to handle. I know you said you know how, but I have to review some safety items with you."

Sam paid attention to Teresa's briefing. It had been a few years since she'd operated the tool, and you never know when you'd learn something.

"Any questions?"

"No," Sam said confidently. She donned her safety glasses, hard hat, ear protection, and gloves and hefted the saw off the ground. It wasn't heavy, but it took a few cuts before she relaxed and fell into a groove. She'd forgotten how much fun it was to operate. She cut up several large trees that had fallen across the roads and hauled what she could out of the way. They'd come back later with the trackhoe and move the heavier pieces.

Sam saw Teresa out of the corner of her eye, so she finished her cut and looked up. When Teresa gave the signal for break time,

Sam nodded and hit the stop button. Even with the ear protection, her ears were ringing.

"Is there anything you can't handle?" Teresa asked, tossing Sam a bottle of cold water.

"A lot of things." Namely my growing attraction to you, she thought. "It's just that so far everything I'm doing I know how to do. Now put me in the kitchen, and I wouldn't get very far."

"Somebody at home cook for you?"

Sam read the meaning under the question. "No. I keep crazy hours, and it's just easier to pick something up on my way home."

"Your job that bad?"

"Not any more than anyone else in my position. But I like to have fun too."

"By doing what?" Teresa asked, appearing interested.

"I race motocross."

"Isn't that driving motorcycles in the dirt?"

"Basically, but we ride specially designed motorcycles in the dirt."

"Sounds like fun. How'd you get started doing that?"

"We used to go to the track and watch my older brother race. I met a girl there, and being young, stupid and in love, I told her that I rode too."

"That's a tough one to talk your way out of."

"I know. I was only twelve, and she was really cute, and I wanted to impress her. Needless to say, I had to learn pretty fast."

"And did she throw herself at you when she saw you on the bike?"

"No. She threw herself at my brother," Sam deadpanned.

Teresa laughed. "Sorry. That's not nice. Probably was awful."

Samantha nodded. "Seems as though I was the only one of the two of us who liked girls. A very one-sided, heartbreaking childhood love affair."

"But you kept at it?"

"Liking girls or riding?"

Teresa's eyes sparkled. "Yes."

"Well. I graduated to women and bigger bikes," Sam said. "I really liked the sport. I got to race against the boys, and I was good at it. It wasn't too much about upper body strength, though I did get pretty buff." Sam jokingly raised her arms in a classic weightlifter stance of flexing her muscles. Teresa squeezed her biceps, sending heat tingling through her.

"Still are," Teresa commented, not yet removing her hand. Far too soon she did.

"One day when I was fifteen, I did meet a girl, and she did throw herself at me. The rest is history, as they say."

"So, riding a dirt bike is a chick magnet?" Teresa asked, grinning.

"To the right kind of chick, yes."

"What else do you do?"

"I love to hang glide."

"Like strap a pair of wings on your back and jump off a cliff?"

"Something like that, yes. An ex took me out a few times, and I got hooked."

"You're quite the thrill seeker," Teresa commented.

"You don't get a second chance to be young, so do it while you can."

"Wise words to live by."

"What about you? What do you do for fun?"

"You're looking at it," Teresa said, pointing to their surroundings.

"You really go from disaster to disaster? All the time?"

"Pretty much."

"Don't you ever get time off? Take a vacation from all of this… destruction? Go to Disney World or someplace fun?"

"I enjoy what I do," Teresa said.

"I do too, but I enjoy not doing it even more."

"Everyone has their own thing," Teresa said, starting to get up. Sam felt Teresa pull away. She might have said the wrong thing.

"Yeah, you're right. Who am I to say? Everyone has their own wants and desires in life. As long as you're happy, that's really all that matters."

But Teresa wasn't as happy as she once was. She'd escaped her old life and built a new one, yet the past year or so she'd felt like something was missing. She worked with the same two or three people at each site, but for the most part she was alone. She had no idea how many people had come and gone in her life during the past seven years. She made a few friends that she kept in touch with through the wonders of technology, but she'd sometimes go months without talking to them. In the places she went, working cell service came in far behind fresh water, electricity, and a safe roof over your head.

It was impossible to have a girlfriend. She never was in one place long enough to do anything more than meet and, if the feeling was mutual, casually hook up. That was all she wanted and certainly all she had the emotional energy for. She'd felt the zing of instant attraction to Sam, yet it was different. She tried not to think about it, but that was next to impossible with Sam lying in the bed next to her. Teresa had woken during the night and watched Sam sleep. She looked peaceful, the rise and fall of her breasts slow and even. She tossed off her covers, indifferent to the heat, her long legs twisted in the sheets. Teresa had imagined them twisted around her legs.

Today watching her handle the chainsaw had been just plain sexy. Teresa loved it when a woman wasn't afraid of hard work. Sam never took any chances when cutting but was quick and efficient. A thin layer of sawdust covered her arms and legs, and she'd had a smudge on her cheek as well.

"What about you?" Sam asked, grabbing her attention again. "Do you have someone that cooks for you at home?"

The face of Molly, her long-time family cook, flashed in Teresa's mind. Her mother had insisted on three balanced meals a day, but Molly always had a plate of cookies hidden in the cupboard whenever Teresa came in. She never understood why Molly kept them hidden. Her mother rarely set foot in the room, let alone opened a cupboard door.

"Nope, not even a cat or a plant."

"You said you have an apartment. Do you go back there often?" Sam asked.

It was a valid question. Normally Teresa would have provided some flippant answer, but instead she said, "No, but it's home, I guess."

Teresa had bought the building her apartment was in and had completely renovated it. She had the entire top floor, the other seven split into four units on each floor. She had priced the units modestly and personally vetted any new tenant. It'd been three months since she'd been there, and when she was at home it took her several weeks to feel like it was home, not just a place to eat and sleep.

Teresa suddenly wanted to show it to Sam. She had refused her mother's insistence that it be professionally decorated and had picked out every piece of furniture, picture, and knickknack herself. Her local friends called it minimalist chic, which was another way of saying it was half empty. She had seen too many people lose everything and not know how to cope.

"I guess you have to have that since you're doing this all the time." Sam gestured to the pile of trees they'd cut. "I have a house with a yard girl, pool girl, and a cleaning lady."

Teresa laughed. "I see a pattern there."

"You know," Sam said, then looked around, her face somber.,"looking at all this, I feel guilty."

"I know what you mean," Teresa said honestly. Her previous lifestyle was so hedonistic it turned her stomach.

"Let's get back at it," Teresa said, looking at her watch. "Lunch is in about an hour or so."

"Great. I'm building up quite an appetite."

Sam stood, her ass directly in Teresa's line of sight.

"So am I," she said.

The chatter around the dinner tables was much the same as it had been the previous evenings. Sam laughed along with everyone at the stories that filled the warm night air. The moon was almost full, providing enough light that lanterns weren't necessary. She was sitting between Dominique and Daniel.

"You know, if lightning were to strike, it wouldn't hit me since I'm sitting between you two."

Daniel laughed, and Dominique shook her head.

"That's all I am—a safety object. And to think I believed you were sitting next to me to enjoy my witty banter."

Sam replied, "Well, there is that."

Laughter caught in her throat when she looked across the fire and locked eyes with Teresa. Even though it was warm, they had built a small fire to keep the bugs at bay. Flames flickered in her eyes, and Sam couldn't look away.

She felt Teresa's gaze on her all day, and Sam had to pay attention to what she was doing or risk serious injury. Their conversation this morning had continued during the break after lunch. Teresa kept things close, preferring to deflect any questions about herself, but Sam had gotten tidbits of information about her. She'd watched her hug one of the neighbor residents, giving her shoulder to cry on, and she tossed the ball to some kids sitting on a pile of rubble. For the short time she'd known Teresa, Sam knew there was much more underneath the easy smile and deflecting words that Teresa didn't want people to see. But she had no doubt what was behind the smoldering look in her eyes now.

If this were another time or place, Sam would walk over, take her hand, and lead her to someplace quiet and private, very private. But she couldn't do that here. Not in front of two dozen people, and for crying out loud, she shared a room with two nuns. Talk about a mood killer.

CHAPTER SIX

Sam didn't know how much more she could take. And worse yet, she didn't know why she wasn't doing something about it. Any other time she'd have put an end to this visual foreplay.

Teresa had experienced another nightmare two nights ago, and Sam had immediately woken and gone to her. Teresa had quieted once Sam stroked her forehead and murmured soft words to her. When Teresa grabbed her hand, Sam held her breath, and it was a few moments before she realized Teresa was still asleep. Sam sat on the side of the bed rubbing the back of her hand until Teresa finally settled down.

Tonight, she had gone in early, preferring to read a little before going to bed. She was sitting in the chair on the other side of the room when Teresa came in.

"Everything all right?"

No, I'm wound so tight, one stroke and I'll explode.

"Yes. I just wanted some time to myself." Dominique and Royale had left earlier in the day to go back to New Jersey.

"Okay. Well, I'll let you be, then." Teresa started toward the door.

"No. That's okay. It's your place too." Sam smiled at her words. She'd almost said it's your house.

"No. I can go. I have some paperwork to do."

"No, really. You don't have to. Unless you're going to play some god-awful music or cook liver."

Teresa smiled and Sam's mouth was suddenly very dry. Teresa had a warm smile and a contagious laugh. Her face lit up and her eyes twinkled. They were doing that now.

"Since I don't have any music and I don't even eat liver, let alone cook it, I think you're safe with me."

No. I'm anything but safe with you, Sam thought.

"What are you reading?" Teresa asked, sitting in the chair next to her.

Sam held the book up so Teresa could see the cover.

"I never would've taken you for a romance reader," Teresa commented.

"It's my go-to-escape place. I read so many technical and financial things my brain fries. I just want to read and relax and not have to think. Besides, who doesn't want a happily-ever-after? I'm kind of a nerd like that, but don't tell my employees. I have a reputation to uphold." Samantha should have felt embarrassed, but she wasn't. Reading lesbian romance was something she hadn't shared with anyone.

Teresa mimicked locking her lips with her fingers. "Your secret is safe with me. Do you want happily-ever-after?"

"Sometimes. But then I like my freedom and doing what I want, when I want. If I want a bowl of cereal for dinner, I eat it. No questions, no arguments, no guilt."

"Do I hear a 'but' in there?"

"No. Not really. Sometimes I'd like to have someone waiting for me when I come home, but it hasn't turned out that way. I'm okay with it."

"Too many women think they can't live without a man, or a woman for that matter."

"I know people like that," Sam said. "Their lives are miserable because of it. My neighbor's husband is a complete ass to her and everyone else, and she won't tell him to hit the road because she doesn't want to be alone. I don't understand it, but I do support her decision."

"Do you have any plans for your day off?" Teresa asked, changing the subject.

Each worker got a day off, and Sam's was approaching.

"The same as I did the last time—sleep," Sam said. She'd never worked so hard and was exhausted, but in a good way.

Again, Teresa smiled. "Everybody says that. It's not like you can go anywhere or do anything. We're in a frigging disaster zone, for crying out loud."

They were silent for a while, and Sam tried to concentrate on her book. Teresa had her eyes closed, her head against the back of the chair. Sam gave up trying to read anything other than the lines on Teresa's face. She looked at peace, a direct contrast to how she appeared when she was having a nightmare. The difference was astounding. Teresa opened her eyes and caught Sam looking.

"Sorry," Sam said, but she wasn't.

"I thought you were reading."

"Lost interest."

"I am disturbing you. I'll go to bed."

Sam wanted to disagree, but Teresa *was* disturbing her, throwing off her perfect life, turning her into someone she almost didn't recognize.

She'd never wanted someone as much as she wanted Teresa. So why wasn't she having her? Why wasn't she following her across the room and into her bed? Why wasn't she exploring her body like she had in her mind this past week? It wasn't because she was her boss. Good grief. This was a volunteer program, not the workplace. Did those rules of behavior even apply? This was different, wasn't it? Surely Teresa thought so. But then again, maybe she didn't. Maybe she thought she'd be seen as taking advantage of their relationship. Sam didn't know what to think. It was obvious Teresa was attracted to her, and the feeling was definitely mutual. Then what the hell? Teresa turned out the light above her head, and Sam picked up her book.

Sam woke to a sound she'd never heard before. She sat up as Teresa thrashed in her bed. Sam's usual technique to calm her didn't work, so she finally crawled under the covers with her. She gathered Teresa in her arms, and after a moment she became still, her breathing back to normal. The bed was big enough for two only if they were intertwined like this or on top of each other. That thought passed through Sam's head, but she didn't dwell on it. The current position was somehow as satisfying as the other would be.

Sex and intimacy were two very different things. One was purely physical, the body's natural reaction to a stimulus. Powerful, yes, absolutely, but still just biology. Intimacy, on the other hand, was complicated. Most people, including Sam, thought sex when they heard the word. But lying here with Teresa in her arms, providing her comfort, was unlike anything she'd ever experienced. It was intimate. She was content and felt at peace.

Those words floated through her subconsciousness until they were right in front of her, so close she could reach out and touch them. This was a moment when she realized she only thought she'd experienced intimacy before.

Teresa shifted closer, and Samantha's hands trembled as she pulled her in. Nothing had ever felt so right. Sam had lain with many women in this same position, but never had it affected her like it did at this moment, and it frightened her. Her friends talked about what it was like when they met "the one," but that was after months of dating and being together. She'd known Teresa for only two weeks. In that amount of time, it had to be lust, plain and simple. A deep emotional connection didn't happen overnight. Good God. This was the first time they'd touched, and it really didn't count because Teresa was asleep. Natural instinct and conscious decision were two very different things. Sam scoffed at her reaction to Teresa. Teresa would obviously feel the same for the same reasons. God, what a mind fuck.

Sam started to disentangle herself to go back to her own bed, but Teresa held her close. She'd give her a few more minutes to settle down, and then she'd leave Teresa's bed. She looked out the window and counted the stars.

CHAPTER SEVEN

It was soft and warm, and whatever it was, Teresa pulled it closer. She was on the precipice of waking and sleeping, afraid that if she woke, the dream would disappear like mist on a rainy day. She didn't want to open her eyes. Didn't want to face another day of being near Sam and not touching her. It was getting harder and harder to stay away from her. They spent almost twenty-four hours a day together, but Teresa wanted to be even closer. She wanted to breathe her air, be inside her, hold her until the sun rose and as it dipped below the horizon every night.

Images of Sam floated through her subconscious. Her smile, her laugh, the way she frowned when she was concentrating. The way she listened to the locals and helped them carry pieces of their lives back to their damaged homes. Sam connected with everyone in the camp, and that was amazing. There were always people who didn't get along, but everyone loved Sam. They engaged her in conversation, and some even asked for her financial advice. She was a natural in this situation. And Teresa wanted her.

She wanted to touch her skin and find out if it was as soft and warm as it looked. Were her kisses as good as her lips were promising? She wanted to know if she made love with as much attention to detail and confidence as she did with everything else. She wanted her hands on her, controlling her like she finessed the big machines every day.

Arousal came into focus and she moved with it. Her hips

moved in time to the rhythmic beating of…Teresa's eyes shot open, but she didn't move.

She was cocooned inside Sam's arms, her hand feeling every beat of Sam's heart. How did she get here? How did Sam get in her bed? What happened?

Teresa was instantly alert. They were both still fully clothed. She didn't feel like she'd had sex, but then again it had been so long she probably wouldn't remember. This definitely didn't feel like the morning after.

She remembered turning off her light and trying to fall asleep. Sam sitting ten feet from her didn't help. Dominique and Royale were a natural deterrent to anything happening between them, and now they were gone. When Sam finally came to bed, Teresa was able to relax and drift off. But how in the hell did they get here?

"You had a bad dream."

Teresa was surprised when Sam spoke. She thought she was still asleep.

"This was the only thing that would calm you down."

Fuck! Teresa never knew her nightmares of that day with the girls was anything other than just in her own head. Dominique and Royale had never said anything, nor had any of the other women that shared the bunkhouse over the years.

Teresa's heart raced. What had she said? Anything that would give her away? Shit, shit, shit! She untangled her arms and legs from Sam's and stood. Her legs were weak at the sight of Sam in her bed. She turned her back to her.

"I'm sorry I disturbed you."

"Don't be. It's okay. I usually fall right back to sleep."

Teresa turned around quickly. "How many times has this happened?" She was desperate to know the specifics but kept her voice calm.

"Once or twice."

Teresa knew Sam was lying. She flushed from anger.

"Don't be embarrassed. We all have bad dreams."

"Is it always like this?" Teresa asked, indicating their position this morning.

"No. Usually you calm right back down."

"After you do what?" Teresa knew Sam wasn't telling her everything. "I want to know."

"I hold your hand and talk to you."

A vague sense of soothing words dashed through Teresa's brain.

"Hold my hand? Like a child?" Teresa couldn't help but be angry. Not at Sam but at herself for allowing someone to see her that way, to see her deepest regrets.

Sam got out of bed, and Teresa couldn't help but look at her bare legs. The ones she was practically humping a few minutes ago. She wasn't sure which scene was worse—her nightmare of the girls being struck by the van or these past few minutes.

"No, not like a child."

Sam stopped in front of her. Her hair was mussed, and she had that just-woke-up look. Teresa's clit pounded, and she cursed inwardly at her body's torturous reactions.

"It's what anyone would've done."

It didn't disturb her as much to know that others might have done the same as it did to know that Sam had. Teresa hated feeling vulnerable, especially with Sam.

Sam stepped closer and cupped her cheek with one hand. Teresa's pulse skyrocketed.

"I don't know what it's about, but I'm willing to listen if you want to talk about it. Whoever Nadia is, she's a very special person."

Teresa was rooted in place as Sam passed her and went into the bathroom. Not only had she seen her nightmare, but Teresa had called out the little girl's name. She grabbed her clothes and ran out the front door before she had to face Sam again.

Chapter Eight

Dinner came and went, with no sign of Teresa anywhere all day. Sam didn't know if she should be worried or angry. No one else seemed to be, so she went with pissed off instead. She wasn't in the bunkhouse, and when Sam woke the next morning, it didn't appear that she'd been there that night. Teresa hadn't said anything about leaving or taking a few days off, and Sam was starting to worry.

"Hi, Mimi," Sam said, catching up to her before she entered her office.

"Samantha, how are you doing?"

"Just fine, thanks. I'm sorry to bother you, but have you seen Teresa?"

"She went to the other side of the island," Mimi said. "She said she had something to take care of and should be back in a couple of days. Do you need something?"

"No. I just hadn't seen her yesterday or last night. I didn't know whether to be worried."

"She's fine. She should have told you, but I guess whatever it was came up suddenly. She probably just forgot. She was anxious to leave."

I'll bet she was, Sam thought, even more angry now.

Two days later, Sam was trying to read when the bunkhouse door opened, and Teresa stepped inside. As angry as Sam still was, Teresa looked wonderful.

"Where in the hell have you been?" Sam said without thinking.

"Hi, honey. I'm home," Teresa said sarcastically.

"Don't hi honey me. I asked you a question. Where have you been?" Sam was surprised at how pissed she still was.

"I was out. I had something I needed to do."

"I know. You were what we call a no-call, no-show for three days. We fire people like that at Bradbury."

"I didn't know I needed to check in with you."

"Don't be obtuse, Teresa."

"Obtuse?"

"Yes, it means—"

"I know what it means," Teresa snapped.

"You could've left word. I was worried."

Something flickered in Teresa's eyes. "Well, you probably got a good night's sleep."

"Stop it," Sam said, springing from her chair. "Is that what this is about? I told you that you have nothing to be embarrassed about."

"You have no business telling me what I can and cannot feel."

"And you have no business leaving me hanging for three days."

"So, because you held my hand and rocked me back to sleep, I owe you something?"

Sam stepped back, stunned by Teresa's words.

"What you owe me is common courtesy," Sam said, regaining control. "And because…" Sam hesitated. She wanted to say, "Because we mean something to each other, and you know it."

"Because what?"

"Because we're in a frigging disaster area, and I was worried," Sam said, using Teresa's words.

"Well, I'm a big girl and can take care of myself."

"That's pretty obvious, and it's also pretty obvious you don't want any help."

"I don't need any help," Teresa said stubbornly.

"Keep telling yourself that."

"And you think you're the one to help me?"

Sam thought about what Dominique had said her first week here. *I think you can help her stop running and forgive herself.*

"Yes, I do," Sam said confidently.

"And why is that? Because we talked over lunch for a few days?"

"Why are you being so ugly to me?" Sam asked.

Her question apparently threw Teresa. She was looking at her as if she was completely confused.

"Why are you being so ugly to me?" Sam repeated.

Teresa's demeanor completely shifted. She went from angry, argumentative, and defensive to defeated in the blink of an eye.

"Because you scare me." Teresa's voice was barely a whisper. Sam wasn't sure she'd heard her correctly.

"I scare you?"

Teresa nodded but didn't look at her.

Sam's anger immediately dissipated. She put her thumb under Teresa's chin and lifted her head. Teresa kept her eyes on the floor.

"Look at me, Teresa." Sam kept her voice soft but firm.

Teresa hesitated, then raised her eyes. They were filled with uncertainty, fear, and vulnerability. Sam's heart pounded. Warning bells were going off in her head. This could not go anywhere, and she could get hurt. She chose to ignore them. *I am in so much trouble.*

"You scare me too."

Sam cupped Teresa's face in her hands and kissed her.

CHAPTER NINE

Teresa's lips were softer than she had imagined, and she savored every sensation. She gently nibbled until Teresa wound her fingers tightly in her hair and pulled her closer, inviting her in for more. They moved into a deep, long kiss, and Sam ran her hands up and down Teresa's back until finally cupping her ass.

She trailed hot, wet kisses across Teresa's face, stopping to nibble her ear lobe. Teresa gasped her pleasure and tightened her grip in Sam's hair. Sensations overwhelmed Sam, and she could barely breathe. Finally, finally, she was where she wanted to be—in Teresa's arms.

Their kisses became more passionate and demanding as Teresa released her hair and tugged at Sam's shirt, not stopping until it was over her head and on the floor. Teresa's wasn't so easy. Sam fumbled with the buttons. She got the first two open, and Teresa reached behind her neck and pulled her shirt over her head. Sam stole a glance at her muscular arms exposed by her tank. It was a toss-up if she wanted to put her mouth back on Teresa's or on her nipples, erect under the thin cotton. Teresa took the decision out of her hands by pulling her to her and kissing her again.

Tongues dueled for advantage while hands tore at their remaining clothes.

"Did you lock the door?" Sam asked, crazy with want. The seconds it took Teresa to step away and throw the lock were far too long, and Sam met her halfway.

Electricity shot through her when their naked bodies touched. Teresa was hot, and a thousand nerve ends reacted. Sam ran her hands over Teresa, not getting enough for her satisfaction.

They stumbled to her bed, and Teresa pulled her down with her. They fit together like they were made to, legs entwined hot and hard against unwavering muscle. Sam reluctantly released Teresa's lips and slid down her chest, closing over a hard nipple.

"God, that feels good." Teresa sighed, pulling Sam's head closer. "Harder," Teresa commanded, and Sam greedily obeyed.

Sam moved to her other breast, her fingers replacing her mouth. She sucked one nipple and tugged on the other as Teresa thrust against her, her warm wetness coating Sam's thigh.

"Jesus, Sam. We'll go slow later. I need you to fuck me. Now." Her voice was husky with desire.

Teresa's words were like throwing gasoline on a fire. Sam didn't waste any time sliding her hand down Teresa's hot, slick body and into her. Teresa cried out and arched her back, digging her fingers into Sam's butt.

Teresa was wet and responsive, and Sam slid her fingers in and out of her wet center.

"Yes, just like that," she said, giving Sam all the directions she needed.

Teresa asked for more and Sam gave it to her. She begged for faster and Sam complied. And when Sam flicked her clit with her thumb, Teresa exploded in her hand.

Sam lifted her head from Teresa's breast to look at her face as she came. It was the most beautiful thing Sam had ever seen. Her face was flushed, her breathing ragged, and a thin layer of sweat shone across her brow. The vulnerability and trust in her eyes was a breathtaking sight. Sam didn't move, afraid she'd break this beautiful moment.

Teresa's grip on her loosened, and Sam started to remove her hand.

"No," Teresa said, putting her hand on top of hers. "Give me a minute," she said after a long shudder.

Teresa was beautiful and Sam kissed her. It was a slow, gentle, passionate kiss but turned heated when Teresa lifted her hips into Sam's hand.

Sam's pulse jumped again, and she decided to make the most of this moment. The first time was fast, the second quick, the third and fourth time slower. They were insatiable for each other, the tension between them simmering like water that had finally come to a boil.

Sam's body was screaming for release, but it would have to wait. There were more important things she wanted to explore with her mouth. Slowly she kissed her way down Teresa, her hand still between her legs.

"God, I like that." Teresa sighed when she nipped her breasts and soothed the spot with her tongue.

"Wait," Teresa said, grabbing Sam's shoulders. Sam lifted her head, swimming with sensation.

"It's your—"

Sam rubbed her fingers on either side of Teresa's clit.

"God, that feels good but—"

Sam added more pressure to her fingers.

"Okay. I see where your interest is at the moment, and since you insist."

Teresa let loose of Sam's shoulders and dropped her legs, giving her complete access. Sam's heart pounded at that one simple action. Teresa knew what was coming next and welcomed it. Sam was definitely not going to turn down the invitation.

She replaced her hand with her tongue and tasted Teresa for the first time. She was sweet and delicious, and Sam took her time exploring. Teresa's hips moved in complete sync with her tongue. Sam looked up Teresa's body and into her eyes. She was propped on her elbows, watching Sam take her. When they glazed over, Sam knew she was close. She pulled her clit into her mouth and sucked.

"Oh my God," Teresa exclaimed, then put her hand over her mouth. Sam felt the pulsing of Teresa's orgasm on her tongue and almost came herself. When Teresa started to move again, Sam eagerly tried something new. This time when Teresa came, Sam was seconds behind her.

Teresa's head was spinning. She had just had the most mind-blowing orgasms of her life and could hardly breathe. Her limbs felt like wet noodles, though she still hummed with energy.

She blinked a few times to focus in the light from the full moon that drifted over the bed. What came into focus next was Sam's mouth still on her. As much as she would like to go again, she wanted Sam worse. She would be selfish in that respect. Her clit twitched in anticipation of getting her hands on Sam. She felt Sam smile against her.

"Oh no, you don't," she said, pushing Sam away. "You can have more of that later. It's my turn."

She pulled Sam up and kissed her, tasting herself on Sam's lips, and rolled her onto her back. They broke apart and laughed as they almost fell out of the narrow bed.

"I feel like I'm back in college," Teresa said as she settled on top of Sam.

"In that case," Sam said, a twinkle in her eye, "your assignment is to make me lose my mind."

"I was always a straight-A student," Teresa countered, enjoying their banter.

"Then I'm sure you'll get an A+," Sam said, pulling Teresa's mouth to hers.

Making love with Sam was unbelievable. She wasn't shy with what she wanted or what she liked. She was responsive and encouraged Teresa with a lift of her hips or a whispered yes. Teresa explored every inch of Sam and several places more than once. She lost track of how many times they climaxed, preferring to focus on the mere fact that she was completely in the moment.

Finally, Sam settled in her arms, and she pulled the sheet over them.

CHAPTER TEN

Sam woke to the sound of running water and lifted her head off the pillow. She was alone, Teresa in the shower. As tempted as she was to join her, two people in that shower was nothing short of dangerous. She loved the feel of Teresa's body pressed against hers, but not in that confined space.

Light was sneaking between the curtains, slashing across the bed where Teresa had lain. Teresa was a passionate, caring, yet demanding lover. She knew just what Sam needed and had Sam grabbing the sheets many times. When Sam thought she couldn't go any further, Teresa coaxed and cajoled her and found more.

Sam was not a one-and-done girl, but she had never had as many orgasms and felt as connected to anyone as she had with Teresa. They were so in tune with each other that for a first time it felt like the hundredth time.

Sam slid into the bathroom to brush her teeth. Teresa was rinsing her hair.

"Good morning. You're up early. I thought you'd sleep till noon," Teresa said, her voice muffled by the running water.

"I'm brushing my teeth, hoping I get lucky instead. Then I'll stay in bed till noon."

Sam couldn't see the expression on Teresa's face clearly, the fog in the small area filling the room.

Sam finished quickly as Teresa turned off the water.

"All yours," she said, shutting the door behind her.

Sam debated what to do. Should she get back into Teresa's bed? Would that be presumptuous? She scoffed. They had just shared each other for hours in the most intimate ways, and it was not presumptuous to assume they'd do it again. God, she certainly hoped so.

Should she go back to her own bed? What would that say? No way would she be able to go back to sleep. Why were mornings-after always so awkward?

Before she could choose, Teresa opened the bathroom door and stepped out. She was wearing a towel that barely covered the places Sam had explored with her hands and her mouth. Even knowing what was underneath, Sam felt her pulse kick up. Her clit throbbed as if it had muscle memory.

"I don't know whether I should climb back into your bed or mine," Sam said, taking the offense against her nerves.

"I, uh," Teresa said, the proverbial deer-in-the-headlights look on her face.

Sam frowned. Had Teresa intended to sneak out before she woke? If so, that was pretty chicken shit, she thought.

"Teresa, I have no illusions of what last night was. We're two unattached, grown women who are obviously attracted to each other. I'm leaving in a week or so, and it's not like I'm going to ask you to give all this up and move to Phoenix to be with me." Sam's stomach dropped when she realized that was exactly what she did want. It churned when she realized it was never going to happen.

She fought to keep her voice steady. "I'm okay with this arrangement as long as you are." God, that sounded so clinical.

Teresa didn't say anything for such a long time that Sam started to get nervous. Finally, she stepped toward her, dropped the towel, and pulled Sam back into her bed.

Sam lay nestled against Teresa, their bodies still warm from their lovemaking. Teresa's heartbeat had almost returned to normal.

"You told me I scared you."

Sam felt Teresa tense.

"Mmm-hmm," she murmured.

"Is that still true?"

Teresa's heart skipped.

"Yes," she whispered.

"Why?"

Sam waited. She had read somewhere that the best way to get someone to talk was to be quiet. People are not comfortable with silence and have a need to fill it.

"Because you make me feel things I've never felt before. You make me want to share everything with you. Things I've never told anyone. Things I'm ashamed of." Her last words were barely audible.

Teresa's heart was pounding, and her breathing hitched. She started to tremble, and Sam's heart cracked a little.

"We all have things we'd do differently if we had the chance. What's important is what we do now." What she said sounded like platitudes, but she didn't know what else to tell her. She was more than a little curious about what Teresa was referring to but knew it was rude to outright ask. They weren't in that type of a relationship.

That was complete bullshit, Sam admitted. She was head-over-heels crazy about Teresa. She wanted the sun, the moon, and the stars with her. She was her happily-ever-after. But that was her side of the relationship. Hell, they weren't in a relationship at all. They were convenient fuck buddies, and the grains of sand in that hourglass were falling through it faster than Sam wanted them to.

"I was a spoiled little rich girl," Teresa said. "No, correct that. I was a spoiled little *very* rich girl. Nobody or nothing was as important as I was. My friends were just like me, and people wanted to be my friend because I was filthy rich. I got whatever I wanted, whenever I wanted it. I was rude and disrespectful and thought my shit didn't stink because I had enough money to pay everybody to say it didn't." Now her voice sounded full of disgust.

Teresa's words stunned Sam. Never would she have imagined the woman in her arms tonight, the woman who worked alongside her in the dirt and muck for the past few weeks, was that same girl Teresa had described.

"Who is Nadia?" Sam knew the woman had to have been the catalyst for the change into the woman she was today.

Teresa's breathing shifted again, and Sam knew she was crying. Sam didn't want to break the spell, and let her speak.

"Nadia was a little girl…"

CHAPTER ELEVEN

T"eresa, I'm glad I caught you," Mimi said as she and Sam stepped out of the bunkhouse. She hoped they didn't have that just-fucked look. But after the past several nights, how could they not?

"What's up?"

"I'll meet you at breakfast," Sam said. "I'm starving." When she passed behind Mimi, she turned around and winked at Teresa. Her knees felt like jelly.

"Three new women are coming in this afternoon. I'll put two of them with you and the other one on the green team."

Teresa's heart sank. That meant the privacy she and Sam had had in the bunkhouse was over.

"Are you okay?" Mimi asked.

"Sure. Great. We need the help," Teresa said truthfully. What was a lie was her enthusiasm for two of the three new women sharing their sleeping quarters.

"Good morning, everyone," Mimi said, clapping her hands to get everyone's attention at the breakfast table. "There's rain in the forecast today, so everybody be extra careful." There were a few moans in the crowd. "We have new volunteers coming in. Three women and four men."

Teresa felt Sam's eyes on her from across the table. When she met them, it was clear Sam had realized the implication. What the hell were they going to do now? Privacy was practically nonexistent in camp, and they certainly couldn't check into a hotel. They were closed due to Eduardo, the son of a bitch.

"…on the blue team with Teresa," Mimi said, pulling Teresa's attention away from the expression on Sam's face.

Fuck!

They didn't have a minute alone all day, and Sam was itching to talk to Teresa. With the new women coming in, did that mean they wouldn't have a repeat of fully exploring each other? No more whispers in the dark and muffled cries of ecstasy? Back to sleeping across from each other? Sam knew she wouldn't be doing much sleeping.

She hadn't even thought that other women would fill the empty beds. It had just never occurred to her. Even after Dominique and Royale left, the thought never crossed her mind. *Yeah, because you couldn't keep your mind off Teresa. And now that you've had her, it's worse. You know what she's like. How she makes you feel. How you soar with pride and power that she has chosen you to touch her. To make her squirm with desire and plead for release. How she…*

"Sam?" Sam blinked a few times to focus. Teresa was standing in front of her.

"Sorry. Daydreaming."

Teresa introduced the two women, and Sam made polite comments and small talk, but resentment grew inside her. Just as suddenly, she realized how selfish that was. These women were here to help this community that needed so much. How—how dare she be pissed they were interrupting her booty call with Teresa?

"I'll catch up with you in a minute," Teresa said to the newbies and turned to Sam. "I'm so sorry. This is not what I wanted."

"Me either. But we need the help."

"We'll figure something out," Teresa said hopefully.

"We better, because I want your hands on me again."

Teresa flushed, and the familiar burn of desire flashed in her eyes.

"Down, girl. You go take care of what you need to do. We'll talk later."

They never had a later, at least not for the next week. The new volunteers knew next to nothing about physical labor, and Teresa felt more like a babysitter than a team lead. She couldn't leave them alone on the job, and it would have been awkward for the two of them to slip off during the evening. With two more women in the bunkhouse, Teresa had no way of knowing who would come in when. A locked door wouldn't have stopped them, as they each had a key. There was no place they could sneak off to while working because Teresa didn't want to have a quick fuck behind a debris pile. Sam was too good for something tawdry like that.

The clock was ticking. Sam was leaving in three days. Seventy-two hours from now she'd be on a plane back to the US.

In the last seven years, women had come and gone out of her life. Some she was glad to see go, some made her sad, and a few more relieved her. Years before that, she really didn't care. Someone else had quickly taken the place of the one who left. But twenty-seven days ago, Samantha Recker had landed on this island, bringing with her strength, perseverance, humility, and compassion. She also brought sunshine, hope, joy, and faith, and Teresa did not want to return to her dull existence. In the past three days she'd come to realize that she was stupid nuts about Sam. Everything about her was a delight and a new experience.

She made Teresa feel whole again when she hadn't even realized she was in pieces. She wanted Sam to stay—on the island and in her life. This was her life now. This was where she belonged. She would never ask Sam to give up her own life. What did she have to offer her? Sam would never trade her yard lady, pool lady, and cleaning lady for living in a bunkhouse with scarce resources and no privacy. Sam was pretty clear about that, with her "no obligation arrangement" speech the morning after.

Teresa was so fucked.

Chapter Twelve

The destruction was still everywhere. What had changed after four weeks was that the ground below Sam looked more organized. Gone was the chaos of trash and debris everywhere. In its place were piles of metal, vegetation, and household goods in neat stacks in key locations as far as she could see. The airport had reopened, and Sam was on one of the few flights out every day. Her backpack was stowed under the seat in front of her, her duffel checked in the cargo hold.

She and Teresa had had no time to be together after the new women arrived. For the past week, she had sensed Teresa pulling back and hesitant to reconnect. The three new women were needy and constantly underfoot and could not be left alone. Finally, one afternoon, a few days ago, Sam found her opportunity.

Teresa was alone in a storage room at the far end of the camp. Everyone was busy, and Sam pulled the door closed behind her. Teresa spun around.

"Hey. I'm in here!" she said before recognizing Sam standing by the door.

"I know, and I've been waiting to be alone with you for days." Sam locked the door and took three steps toward Teresa. Teresa put her hands up to stop her.

"Sam, I don't want to do this here," she said, looking around them. The shelves were filled with canned goods and relief supplies.

"Why not?" Sam asked, her heart sinking. Why had she not seen the clues that Teresa didn't want a repeat?

"Because you're too good for a quick fuck in a supply room."

Sam's disappointment disappeared, replaced with the desire that had threatened to overpower her these last few days.

"If this is the only place I can get my hands on you, I don't care." She stepped closer, stopping just as their breasts touched. "And who said it was going to be quick?"

That had been their last time together. Samantha left the next day.

She fingered the beaded necklace around her neck, remembering the people on the island who had welcomed her. Never had she felt so needed and so fulfilled by giving her time and what little skill she had. She was touched deep down by this experience and knew she would carry it with her every day. Sam also knew she'd also left a part of her behind in the arms of a tall, dark-haired beauty.

End of Part I

PART II

Jamaican Haven

Cora and Tyler

Chapter One

Cora wished she were at least six inches taller. Ten would be awesome, but she'd take four. At barely five feet tall, she was forever at a disadvantage. People thought she was twelve instead of thirty-eight, the clothes in the petite section made her look like a Barbie doll, shoes were next to impossible to find, and, until they invented gas and brake pedals that adjusted, the steering wheel was far too close to her chest. Equally disturbing, it was impossible to stow her luggage in the overhead compartment on a plane without asking for help, and she asked only when she absolutely had no other alternative.

Cora shoved her carry-on under the seat in front of her and settled in for the nine-hour flight to Jamaica. She was not in first class because of the extra legroom, because she certainly didn't need it, but because it was quieter, and she wouldn't be bombarded by people talking, kids squawking, and her neighbors bumping her on the way to the bathroom.

"Business or pleasure?"

"Excuse me?"

"Business or pleasure?" The woman sitting beside her in the window seat was a little younger than her, maybe in her late twenties, and was what her sister would call devilishly attractive.

"By the looks of the people boarding and our destination, I'd say everyone is going on vacation."

The woman smiled at Cora as she waited for an answer. The flight attendant stopped and took their drink orders.

"Both."

"What is your business?"

"I work for a construction firm."

"Are you building something in Kingston?" the woman asked, naming their destination city.

"No. I'm going to do some volunteer work."

The woman smiled again, and this time she winked at Cora.

"And flying first class to boot. Some volunteer work."

Cora's father always used that phrase—"to boot." What did it even mean? Was it one word or two? Was the "to" spelled "too" or "two"?

"I'm Ford Stewart," she said, extending her hand. "I know," she said ruefully. "My dad loved cars and wanted a boy."

Cora had no interest in talking to the woman for hours, but to not shake her offered hand would just be plain rude. Cora might not be an extrovert or a witty conversationalist, but she wasn't rude.

"Cora."

The way Ford was looking at her made Cora start getting lesbian vibes. That was interesting, but what was the point? They'd be on a plane, then go their separate ways. On second thought, that was a very good point—the part about going their separate ways afterward. This might be a very interesting flight.

Cora wasn't socially awkward, but she rarely started a conversation. She was comfortable with and by herself, and she hated meeting people for the first time. Small talk didn't come naturally to her. Several years ago, when she first started working at Bradbury, her boss, Addison, took her under her wing and gave her a piece of advice. She told her to have at least ten things prepared to talk about when you meet someone. The same ten questions might or might not be asked at a dinner party and a business conference. Addison had been aghast when Cora confessed that she could go to a three-day meeting and not say a word to another person and be completely happy. She'd even go so far as to skip the free lunch because she had absolutely no desire to sit elbow-to-elbow with nine complete strangers.

Cora hustled down to baggage claim because her quick detour to a private suite in the executive club with Ford had ended up being anything but quick. She hoped her luggage was still there. She could just imagine how she would explain that to the customer-service representative at the lost-luggage counter.

"I went into one of the private suites with a woman I met on the plane, and I was otherwise preoccupied with several mind-blowing orgasms so I couldn't get down here in time. You know how it is." She probably wouldn't say that to the volunteer coordinator, or anyone else for that matter, when she showed up without any luggage. She'd simply say, "When I got to baggage claim, my suitcase wasn't there." Completely the truth.

The carousel had stopped turning, and her bag was sitting like a lone occupant on a playground merry-go-round. She sighed with relief, pulled it off, and went to find the rental-car counter.

Cora had never done anything like that before, but hell, she was on vacation. Some would say it was dangerously stupid, but lately she was feeling an overwhelming need for a change. She was a creature of habit: the same two or three things for breakfast, lunch at her desk, the gym after work and on Saturday. She had a few close friends, and they got together occasionally.

Cora had often been described as quiet. She just thought that if it wasn't important enough to say, then don't say it. She preferred to observe, and she had fine-tuned that skill to perfection. She could read body language as well as detect subtle shifts in tone, eye connection, and demeanor, and because of those abilities, she was an expert negotiator, which was her job.

She was not the life of the party even if she went to a party. She hated even going unless she knew several people there. It was at one such party that she had discovered fan fiction.

She instantly become curious and had done more than a little research and tiptoed in. Now, a year later, she had a large following. Cora had a pen name and wrote what she called futuristic fiction. It wasn't sci-fi with other worlds and creatures but life one hundred years from now. Not too bizarre or far out there. She'd never had a creative cell in her brain until she put pen to paper. The stories poured out of her in a flood of words that so far had yet to end.

Maybe that was what had unleashed the sense of adventure she'd never had. She traded in her conservative four-door sedan for an F150 four-wheel-drive pickup truck, bought a mountain bike and camp trailer, and went camping almost every weekend. She canceled her yard and pool service and discovered how proud she felt when she looked at the tangible finished products she herself had accomplished. She came to work on Mondays with an outdoor glow and bandages on her scrapes and scratches. At times she didn't recognize herself.

Cora had rented a condo in Kingston for the month she was going to be on the island. She had no desire to stay cooped up in a hotel. That would feel too much like she was just traveling for work, which was the last thing she wanted to do. The island of Jamaica, located about ninety miles south of Cuba, was one hundred and forty-five miles long and fifty miles wide. Over two million people called it home. Kingston was a bustling metropolis with popular beaches, shopping, and nightlife. There was plenty to do for the more than four million tourists that landed on the island each year. When she wasn't volunteering, Cora was looking forward to putting her toes in the sand, soaking up the sun, and enjoying the reggae beats of the island. In other words, simply relaxing and unwinding.

Chapter Two

"Tyler, what in the hell are you doing? You're going to get yourself killed."

"I'll be fine. Just a little bit farther…" Tyler held on to the branch with one hand and leaned over the canal. It had rained over a dozen inches the past few days, and the water was moving swiftly. She was almost there, just a few more inches and…

"Shit!"

"Tyler!"

The water was cold, and it took Tyler's breath away. She came up sputtering and, once she got her bearings, looked around for the dog she and Olivia had seen on their morning run. Somehow it had gotten stuck in the branches of a tree growing next to the canal.

Tyler had just wrapped her fingers around the scruff of the dog's neck when the branch broke, and she and the scruffy dog tumbled into the water.

The dog was about ten yards in front of her, struggling to keep his head above the water. She quickly swam to catch up to it.

As she got closer, she used her best "It's okay, you're going to be fine. I'm here to help you" voice, even though her teeth were chattering. The dog turned toward the voice, terror in its eyes. This was going to be tricky, she thought. Dogs bite if they're scared, and this one was terrified. That, combined with the rushing water that was far too deep for Tyler to stand up in, did not bode well for a good outcome. At a minimum she'd get bit. With luck, they would both get out unscathed.

She reached out and grabbed the dog around the middle, narrowly missing having it bite off her ear. Tyler had been rescuing animals from the streets of Jamaica for over fifteen years and had the scars to prove it. As she looked for a way out of the rain-swollen canal, she hoped this rescue wouldn't add to them. The water was rough, and she scraped her arms and legs on the cement walls when she reached for something to try to grab on to.

The force of the current and the squirming dog took her under several times, and she coughed and sputtered as she inhaled dirty water. The last time she went under she wasn't sure she'd come back up, but then she felt strong arms pull her to the surface.

"Tyler, one of these days you're going to get yourself killed."

They had dropped the dog off at the shelter, her friend Olivia insisting the volunteers take care of her. Tyler came home with her.

"It wasn't that bad, Olivia." It was, but Tyler would never admit it.

"The hell it wasn't," Olivia replied, her hands on her hips, a frown creasing her forehead.

"Is that your mean-teacher stance?" Tyler asked, trying to deflect Olivia's anger.

"Yes, and don't change the subject on me. I wrangle twenty-eight first-graders five days a week. Nothing gets by me. Your teeth are still chattering, and you haven't stopped shivering. One of these days your penchant for rescuing every animal you see will get you killed."

"Olivia, please. You've said the word 'killed' three times today. I get it. But I couldn't leave her there. She would have died."

"And you almost did. I would have been really pissed off to lose my running partner."

In addition to that, Olivia was Tyler's best friend and confidante. They'd been close for a little more than five years when Olivia brought her class to visit Haven, the shelter Tyler had established four years earlier. They were there on a community-service field trip to feed, clean up, and play with the animals. Three hours later, Tyler had a new friend, and the kids had more poo on their shoes than in the poop-scoop bag.

"Here, drink this." Olivia handed her a cup of hot tea. "I'll put your clothes in the wash."

Tyler shivered again and almost spilled her tea. Maybe Olivia was right. Maybe it hadn't been a smart idea to try to climb down the tree and rescue the dog. But no way could she leave any animal in distress.

Olivia came back into the room. "How are you feeling?"

"Better," Tyler lied.

"That was the stupidest thing you've ever done."

"No, it wasn't." But what Olivia didn't know wouldn't hurt her.

"You're lucky that electric truck was in the alley."

According to Olivia, she had run along the canal as the fast current pushed Tyler farther away from her. She had caught the attention of an electric worker, who'd tied a rope to his waist and jumped in after her.

The dog did bite Tyler, but she hadn't told anyone. At the time she didn't think it was too bad, but now that her adrenaline had started to wane, her hand was throbbing and dripping blood on Olivia's floor.

"What the fuck, Tyler!" Olivia ran across the room. Tyler flinched when she took her hand.

"Jesus Christ, Tyler, she bit you. Why didn't you say something?"

Olivia wrapped her hand in a towel she grabbed from the kitchen counter.

"Don't move," she said before she left the room.

Tyler's head was spinning, and black dots flashed in front of her eyes.

❖

Tyler recognized the chain on the ceiling fan in Olivia's bedroom, which wobbled as the blades slowly turned above her. What was she doing in Olivia's bed?

"You've got to stop doing that."

"What?" Tyler croaked, her throat dry.

"Scaring the shit out of me. Twice in one day is two times too many."

"What, what happened?" Tyler was groggy and tried to sit up.

"Whoa. You fainted. You need to lie still for a while."

Olivia put her hand on Tyler's shoulder and pushed her back on to the bed. Tyler closed her eyes, and the world stopped spinning.

Later, when she opened them again, Olivia was sitting beside her in the bed reading a book. She was old-school like that.

"Hey." Tyler's lips felt chapped.

"Hey, sleepyhead. How are you feeling?" Olivia put her hand on Tyler's forehead.

"Better, I think." This time Tyler was telling the truth.

Olivia left and came back with a glass of water. Tyler sat up.

"If you wanted to be in my bed, Tyler, all you had to do was ask." They teased each other all the time, though neither of them was the slightest bit serious.

"Do you want me to ask?" Tyler sipped the cool water.

"Absolutely not. You're queer and my best friend. Both off-limits in my book."

"I bet you say that to all your queer best friends."

"Busted," Olivia said, nudging Tyler with her shoulder.

It felt good to laugh with Olivia. They often shared a few beers and swapped stories about their week.

Olivia owned a gallery popular with both the locals and tourists that specialized in wildlife and nature photos, but she also had a large demand for her landscapes. Tyler had three of them mounted on the walls in her house.

"Seriously, Tyler, you need to think before you chase some stray animal. One of these days your nine lives will run out."

Tyler was known in animal-rescue circles as someone who would do anything to save an animal. She'd spent hours wedged inside a pipe trying to reach a litter of kittens. She set humane traps all over the island to safely catch stray dogs and cats. One time she was on her way to her sister's wedding and saw several puppies run across the road and disappear into the trees. She was almost late for her bridesmaid duties and was featured in the local news magazine. A few months ago, a camera crew from a nationally syndicated morning show had followed her around for a week for a feature story.

"You're starting to sound like my mother."

"Well, you know what they say. Mother always knows best."

Tyler pushed the covers back and swung her legs over the side of the bed, then rose slowly just in case she got dizzy again.

"I've had enough fun for one day. I think I'll head home." Her running clothes were folded neatly on Olivia's dresser.

Tyler suppressed a moan of pain as she walked to the dresser. She slid the shorts Olivia had given her down her legs and gingerly stepped out of them. Then she carefully stepped into hers and repeated the same with her sports bra and tank.

Olivia pointed to the white gauze bandages on her arms and legs.

"You need to change those bandages before you go to bed tonight and first thing tomorrow morning. And keep that hand dry for a few days," she said, indicating her bandaged left hand.

"Yes, Mother." Tyler knew she sounded like a teenager humoring a clueless parent.

"And you better be going home and not to the shelter to check on the dog. Evelyn called me. She's fine, and they named her Agua."

"Yes, dear. I am headed home." *After I check on Agua.*

CHAPTER THREE

Cora arrived at Haven a little after eight, eager to start. She'd be at the rescue shelter for just about four weeks, doing whatever they needed her to do. In addition to her time, Bradbury Construction had donated funds to cover the cost for twenty new indoor/outdoor kennels and a new exercise yard.

Haven was located in a converted old warehouse and sat on six acres adjacent to an industrial park. The first floor of the building held the main areas of the shelter, including an intake area, medical center, grooming area, kennels, and the reception area. The second floor housed the administrative offices.

She pushed through the first set of doors, then the second to enter the lobby. A very thin man with a full, dark beard sat behind a large desk directly in front of her.

"Welcome to Haven. Can I help you?"

Cora approached the desk, the sound of barking dogs to her left.

"I'm Cora Donaldson. I'm volunteering for several weeks."

The man jumped up and hurried around the desk.

"Yes, Miss Donaldson. We're expecting you. We're so happy to have you with us."

And our cash, Cora thought, then felt the heat of embarrassment for her cynical attitude.

"I'm excited to be here too."

"I'm Michael, and I have some papers for you to sign. Then

we can get you started." He bustled around behind the counter and handed Cora a clipboard and a pen.

Paperwork complete, Michael gave her a tour, introducing her to the handful of paid staff and the other volunteers. Even though she hated meeting new people, surprisingly she immediately clicked with everyone.

"Tyler was here earlier," Michael said, waving toward an open door to an office as they passed by.

Cora peeked inside. A battered desk was cluttered with paperwork, a couple of leashes, and a container of colorful treats. A pair of muddy rubber boots sat in the corner, along with a pair of jeans and a rain slicker hanging on a coat rack. The chairs in front of the desk were old but serviceable. A blanket was tossed on a small couch against the far wall. Donations were not spent decorating this office.

As the tour continued, Cora was impressed with the neatness and cleanliness of every area of the shelter. Medical was spotless and smelled of disinfectant, the stainless-steel surfaces gleaming.

"Three veterinarians work with us. One is always on call. Every animal that comes in gets a thorough exam and evaluation and a case plan developed."

"A case plan?"

"It's a complete detail of their history and what we're planning to do with them. Most times the history is only one paragraph, about the conditions in which we found them. It also contains their medical and social evaluation and the developed action plan, which is very specific. Every worker is expected to know the plan for any animal they encounter. We work hard to get these animals into a good home and try to see that every one of them that needs extensive therapy gets it. One wrong move and they could be set back weeks of work. This is the intake area."

Cora stepped into a room already crowded with six people.

"This is the dog that came in this morning," Michael said, his voice quiet.

A medium-sized black dog was sitting on the stainless-steel exam table, a large, fluffy towel underneath it.

"What's her story?" Cora just assumed it was a female.

"Tyler and Olivia found her in one of our canals during their morning run. Tyler fell in trying to get her, and they both had to be fished out."

"Why is she muzzled?" Cora knew very little about dogs, which was another reason she'd chose this place.

"She bit Tyler."

"She looks terrified." Cora felt for the scruffy dog trembling on the table.

"They usually are when they come in. Some of these animals have been wild their entire lives. Others have never had a good experience with a human. They're aggressive simply to defend themselves or scared to death like this girl. Either way, biting is quite common. We'll get her out of that muzzle as soon as we complete the intake exam. We use it only as a last resort for our protection or the protection of other animals."

"Excuse me," a woman said, brushing past Cora and hurrying into the room. "How is she?" the woman asked, more than a little concern in her voice.

As the team briefed her, Cora got a better look at the woman.

"That's Tyler," Michael whispered to her.

Tyler was quite a bit taller than Cora, but who wasn't? A pair of long, muscular legs spilled out of the bottom of tight running shorts that fit very nicely over an equally nice ass. Her blue racerback top exposed well-defined shoulders and arms, her native skin looked smooth, and her accent, when she spoke, was just plain sexy. Her dad would have called her a tall drink of water. From this view Tyler was mouthwatering.

Down, girl, Cora thought as she glanced at her watch. You're not twenty-four hours from having your hands on and in a total stranger, and you're already thinking about someone else. Maybe Miss Ford had kick-started her dormant libido. Cora hadn't had a steady girlfriend for several years, and the occasional hookup relieved her pent-up stress. Today, however, it was apparent that it hadn't sated it but whetted it. As attractive as Tyler was, she shouldn't have her hand in that treat jar. Cora always kept her work and personal life separate.

"Let me show you the outdoor area," Michael said as they left the room.

Regardless of what Cora had just told herself, she had a hard time breaking away from practically staring at Tyler Sanchez.

❖

"Are you even supposed to be here?" Tyler knew that Evelyn, her shelter manager, was going to seriously scold her.

"I heard Olivia tell you not to come back here and that we would take care of Agua."

Evelyn was a sixty-year-old grandmother who ran the shelter like she ran her command as a US Army officer. Tyler hired Evelyn when she came into the shelter looking for something to do, saying that retirement was for the dead.

"It's on my way home," Tyler said before Evelyn interrupted her.

"I don't care if you live upstairs. You do not need to be here. You need to be home in bed."

"I don't need to be in bed," Tyler said. Well, I do, but not for this, she thought. Even though she and Evelyn had become good friends outside of work and would make a comment like that over a beer, she would never cross that line at work.

"Geez, is everybody my mother? She wouldn't be pleased for you and Olivia to usurp her job."

"Wow, *usurp*. That's a big word for a girl who fell out of a tree this morning," Evelyn said, shaking her head. "Go home, pop some Advil, and take a nap. Agua will be fine, and you know it." Evelyn took Tyler by the shoulders, turned her around, and gently pushed her toward the staff entrance. "I do not want to see you until tomorrow, or you will not be happy."

Evelyn was right. Tyler had attracted a great group of people who knew what they were doing. Donations had never been higher, and she was starting to see some positive results from her halfway house. Not wanting to suffer any more of Evelyn's wrath, Tyler exited through the staff entrance but changed direction from her truck to the back gate of the yard area. The water pressure of the pond pump had been acting up lately, and she needed to get today's reading. She punched in the six-digit code to unlock the gate, which had started sticking lately, so she gave it a strong tug.

The gate swung open far too easily, and Tyler stumbled backward. Someone was pushing on the gate and fell into her, knocking both of them to the ground. Tyler hit first, followed by the other person, followed by an entire bucket of poo.

Chapter Four

O h my God. "I'm so sorry," Cora said automatically.
       Michael had told her to push hard on the gate, and her momentum had driven her forward into a soft wall of flesh before they both toppled to the ground. Cora caught her breath when she found herself looking into the dark eyes of none other than Tyler Sanchez.

Tyler's body was soft under hers, and they fit together amazingly well. Her muscle memory from yesterday morning kicked in, and she immediately shifted for closer contact. Tyler's eyes opened wide, and her eyebrows shot up.

Tyler's eyes were dark blue and mesmerizing. Cora wanted to drown in them and for no one to throw her a lifeline. Tyler shifted, and a jolt of desire shot through Cora. The reaction must've been reflected in her eyes, because Tyler's immediately smoldered.

"I usually like to get at least a woman's name before we're in this position." Tyler's eyes sparkled, her voice deep and smooth. Cora tingled all the way down to her toes. She was tongue-tied, but before she had a chance to say anything, Tyler's face scrunched up.

"What is that smell?"

Just then the overwhelming scent of dog poo assailed Cora. The poo bucket! She'd volunteered to police the area, and Michael had told her to drop it all in the large waste container just outside the back gate. Cora gasped, then started coughing. Not a good idea. She scrambled to her feet.

"Shit. No, I mean, yes. No, I mean, I'm so sorry," she said as she held out her hand to help Tyler up. Tyler looked at it, probably to make sure it was poo-free. Cora wiped it on her shorts just to be safe.

"I'm sorry," she said for the third time. "Michael told me to push hard on the gate, but I wasn't expecting somebody to be pulling on it at the same time."

Tyler took her hand and stood.

"Well, this is an introduction neither one of us will forget. I'm Tyler Sanchez."

"Cora Donaldson."

"I don't think I've ever seen you here, Cora."

"It's my first day."

"And a very memorable one at that, wouldn't you say?"

Tyler was still holding her hand, and Cora felt warm all over, though not from the sun overhead.

"I know I'll never forget it," Cora commented, knowing just how true that was.

"Nor will I," Tyler said, then let go of her hand. Cora's immediately felt cool and very empty.

"Let me help you with this." Tyler started to pick up the bucket, but Cora started.

"No!" Cora shouted, mortified as it was. "It was my fault. I'll get it. You go on and do whatever you were going to do before I dumped poo all over you." Cora groaned.

Tyler looked down at her soiled clothes. "I think I'll take a rain check and just head home. You probably should too. Michael can find you a pair of scrubs to wear."

"I'm not going home. I'm staying at a house I rented on the beach, but I guess it kind of is home." *Shut up, Cora. You're rambling.* She never rambled.

"On the beach?" Tyler asked. "Very nice. Are you from the US?"

"Yes."

"Here on vacation?"

"Yes and no. I'll be working here for a few weeks."

"Lucky us. And you're staying at the beach to enjoy on your time off. Even better."

They stood there looking at each other, the electricity crackling in the hot afternoon. Cora wanted to say so many things. Would you like to meet me for a drink later? Dinner? Sleepover?

Tyler must have been thinking similar thoughts, because her eyes darkened, and desire smoldered just a bit in them. A few moments ago, they were standing close enough to kiss, and Cora's natural instinct was to do just that. Damn her ethics!

"Oh my God, you're bleeding," Cora said, pointing at Tyler's leg. Blood was dripping down her leg, the bandage soaked with it.

Tyler looked at her leg and shook her head. "It's nothing, just a little abrasion," she said dismissively.

Cora pointed at it and Tyler's other bandages. "That doesn't look like a little anything. Did you get that when you rescued the dog I saw earlier?"

"You saw her?"

"Just for a moment. After I signed all the paperwork, Michael gave me a tour. She was in the intake room, and you came in to check on her. He told me what you did…to save her." Cora stopped, again uncharacteristically rambling.

"I didn't see you." Tyler seemed disappointed and appeared thoughtful, as if trying to remember the detail of the scene.

"Well, I'm sorry for being rude and not introducing myself. I can get a little caught up with an animal." Tyler blushed at what she must think was her own shortcoming.

"That's completely understandable. How is she, by the way?"

"A little scared but really sweet. She didn't have a collar, so we'll have to try to track down her owner."

"She didn't have a chip?" Cora asked, referencing the tracking chip placed just under an animal's skin. When a stray is found, the chip can be scanned and the owner's information read on a screen.

"Unfortunately, unlike in the US, chips aren't widely used here, and most of the animals we rescue have never had a home."

Cora looked at Tyler's bleeding leg again. "You'd better take care of that, and I better get this cleaned up, or they might fire me on my first day," she said nervously, gesturing to the poo on the ground.

Tyler gazed at her and smiled. "I'm the boss. Nobody's going to fire you."

Chapter Five

Tyler finally went home, tossed her clothes into the washer, and took a quick shower, changing her bandages. Her injuries hurt like hell, and it had been hard to wash her hair with one hand. She had just sat down with a glass of wine after dinner when Evelyn called.

"Who is Cora?" The image of a petite yet fiery redhead came to mind.

"Hello to you too," Evelyn said.

"Yes, hello, Evelyn. So, who is Cora? I ran into her at the shelter today."

"She's one of our new volunteers. She's with Bradbury Construction. She'll be with us four days a week for a month."

"A month?" How in the hell was she going to keep her hands off Cora for a month? Wait, no. If she worked four days a week, times four weeks, that was only sixteen days. Tyler admitted she'd just have to take it one day at a time. Based on her body's reaction to Cora on top of her, that was going to be easier said than done.

"When did you run into her?" Evelyn asked suspiciously.

Why did I hire her again, Tyler asked herself.

"On my way to my truck." Not a lie.

"She doesn't want any special treatment, which is almost comical since her company is financing our new kennels. Obviously, we're not going to have her poop-scoop."

"Well, Michael didn't get that message, because when I saw her, she had a very full bucket." *Had* being the operative word.

Evelyn sighed. "I'll talk to him. He's not the most politically savvy."

"No, don't. If she wants to be a typical volunteer, let's honor her wishes." Tyler, however, wanted to treat her very special.

They chatted for a few more minutes, and Evelyn relayed that Agua was resting quietly in her kennel. Tyler hung up and immediately continued to think about Cora. She'd first thought when she saw her with Michael that she was somebody's little sister he was giving a tour. Granted, she didn't know who she was when she passed her on her way into the treatment room. But after feeling her very grown-up body on hers, she hoped she was nobody's sister, big or little.

Tyler chuckled, remembering Cora's expression when she realized she'd dumped the entire bucket of poo on them. Did she actually think Tyler would fire her? It was an accident. But more disturbing, which wasn't an accident, was the chemical reaction between them. She certainly felt it and was sure Cora had as well.

Tyler couldn't remember ever experiencing that kind of immediate reaction to someone. Of course, she'd never met someone for the first time in such an intimate position. Even after getting to know a woman, she'd never felt like this. Go figure it would be someone at work.

Tyler had spent most of her adult life rescuing lost and forgotten animals. She'd started out with a stray or two, but as she rescued more and more, she'd needed a place to house them. She had tapped out all her friends and family to foster an animal or three, and the need far exceeded the capacity. She'd stumbled upon the old warehouse one day as she was looking for a costume rental shop. She had gotten turned around and stopped in front of the building to get her bearings. A for-sale sign, rusted from age, was screwed into an old metal door. It was obvious the building hadn't been occupied for many years. Just for giggles, Tyler had dialed the number that she could barely see on the sign.

Two months later she'd rounded up every family member,

friend, and acquaintance she had and set to work rehabbing the structure. She'd had bought the building at a very low price, the realty company wanting to unload it. She had sold her house, moved into the empty building, ate nothing but sandwiches, never went out and had a beer, and sold her grandmother's pearl brooch to fund what she now knew was her true calling. As much as she would love to quit her job and rescue and rehabilitate animals full time, she had bills to pay, supplies to buy, and facilities to maintain. Her day job kept them afloat until she'd started making a name for Haven and donations had begun to come in. Haven was not turning a profit, but it took in what it needed, with some to spare for extras.

Tyler realized it wasn't smart to get involved with anyone who worked or volunteered at Haven. That was just not good for business or her future. Too many times she'd seen coworkers get involved, and when it ended, things often got really messy. The boss-subordinate relationship was not cool, and she'd never even been tempted to hook up with one of the many volunteers that came in and out of Haven.

The phone rang. Tyler's sister was on the other end. Tyler settled on her couch, getting comfortable.

"Hey, Gabrielle." Gabrielle and Tyler had been born within minutes of each other, Gabrielle claiming the role as older sister whenever it suited her. They got along as twins almost always do, a powerful sixth-sense connection between them. If one of them was hurting, the other felt it. When Tyler had broken her arm three years ago, Gabrielle knew and called her almost immediately. They were close, Gabrielle investing some of her hard-earned money as a hairstylist in Haven. Currently she was fostering two dogs and a cat.

"Hey, Tyler. What's new?"

They talked almost every day, but Tyler had been so busy lately with a real-work project and getting ready for the construction to begin on the shelter, it had been almost a week since she'd heard her sister's voice.

"Same thing. Work, rescue, rinse, repeat."

"You start construction this week, right?"

"Yes, on Wednesday."

"You have got to be so excited. This is a big deal, Tyler. I am so proud of you." Not only was Gabrielle her sister, but she was also her biggest supporter.

"I know. We've been waiting so long for this, sometimes I can't believe it's happening."

"Mama and Papa would be so happy for you."

Their parents, along with a neighbor, had been killed by a drunk driver twelve years earlier on their way home from dinner.

"I feel them, Gab. Every day, I feel them all around me." The agony of losing her parents had subsided. It wasn't still a sharp, debilitating pain, but more of a dull ache where a big piece of her heart had once been. She and Gabrielle hadn't left each other's side for the first six months, grieving and drawing strength from each other.

"I know. I do too, Tyler. I swear I see Papa in everything Tito does." Tito was Gabrielle's three-year-old son and a carbon copy of their father. Every time Tyler saw her nephew was painful yet heartwarming.

"Did that lady that works for the firm that gave you the money arrive? What was her name again?"

"Cora Donaldson. Yes. Today was her first day." Tyler had known someone from Bradbury Construction was coming, but she'd left the details to Evelyn. She'd been surprised when it was Cora.

"What's she like? A snooty American?"

Cora was hardly what Tyler would classify as a snooty American. She was American, yes, but even from their brief interaction, Tyler sensed that she was kind, caring, and compassionate toward animals. Over the years, Tyler had developed an instinct regarding who was good with animals and who simply went through the motions. When Cora had inquired about the stray, she knew she'd been right.

"No. Not at all. I don't think she's any taller than a meter and a half and has red hair and green eyes." They always joked about the typical American woman.

"How long is she there for?"

Tyler heard Tito squealing in the background.

"A month or so. Tell Tito Aunty Tyler said it's time for bed."

"It's been time for bed for over an hour. It's François's turn. I gave up. I have only one child. I don't know how Mama did it with two."

"She spanked our butts is how she did it." Tyler and Gabrielle laughed and reminisced about their mother for a few minutes.

Tyler goaded her sister. "She loved me more."

"That's only because when you told her you were a lesbian, she thought she hadn't given you enough love," Gabrielle said in a teasing tone.

That was the farthest from the truth. On the very rare occasion Tyler brought a woman to a family function, her parents had welcomed her with open arms.

"Speaking about lesbians, you never answered me about the woman with the money."

Tyler laughed. "First of all, *she* does not have the money. She works for the company that donated it, and how did you transition from my coming out to Cora?" Tyler asked, already knowing the answer.

"Please, Tyler. When will you learn that I, as the older sister, know everything. You can hide nothing from me. And I mean nothing. So don't even try."

"Why do I even bother?" Tyler acquiesced, still dumbfounded at times how her sister did it. No sense fighting it. "Cora is going to be here about four weeks."

"That'll give you plenty of time," Gabrielle commented, then said something to her husband.

"Time for what?"

"To get her in bed."

"Gabrielle, you know I don't mess with anyone I work with." However, the thought had crossed her mind several times since she met Cora. "That's just not smart. And I did get the brains in the family," Tyler added.

"And all the lesbian sex appeal, which is fine by me. I'll take the other side. I have to go. François has no clue how to get a defiant toddler to stay in bed. Call me after you break ground. I want to hear all about it. And definitely after you kiss Cora. Bye."

Tyler was still laughing and thinking about how she could obey her sister's orders as she pushed the end button on her phone.

CHAPTER SIX

"And then I dumped a bucket of dog shit on her." What had happened still sounded unbelievable to Cora, even hours later.

"Jesus, Cora. You sure know how to make a first impression."

"That's exactly what she said. I'm telling you, Jenny, I could've crawled under a speck of dirt I was so embarrassed."

Jenny Frame bought the house next to Cora a month after she moved in and, only due to Jenny's persistence, they had ended up being good friends. Jenny had insisted Cora call her after her first day at the shelter.

"So, are they going to let you come back tomorrow?"

"Tyler said I didn't have to worry about being fired because she's the boss."

"She as good-looking as in her pictures?"

Cora had shown Jenny the articles about Tyler and the shelter when she'd decided that was where she was going. They both had commented about how hot Tyler was.

"Not in the slightest. Pictures do not do that woman justice." It had only been a few hours since she met Tyler, and Cora still hummed all over just thinking about her. If she believed in love at first sight, this would be it. Every time they touched, a current passed through Cora that she couldn't ignore. Even when Tyler had brushed by her on her way into the intake room, she'd felt something though she hadn't even known who Tyler was. The attraction was exciting but scared the hell out of her. She'd have to be very careful around her.

"Do tell." Jenny prompted her.

"She's really tall, probably close to six feet, and she has an energy about her that fills the room. Her hair is jet-black, and her eyes are the most riveting shade of blue I've ever seen. Her accent is not too strong and has a touch of British. It's kind of like warm butter."

"Sounds like somebody's got the hots for her boss."

That was an understatement, Cora thought. "Another place, another time, and I'd be all over her."

"Speaking about all over her," Jenny said, "tell me again about the woman from the plane. What was her name again? Chevy? Toyota?"

Cora laughed, and as she finished another glass of wine, she and Jenny swapped sex stories.

The next morning Cora stood in front of the closet trying to decide what to wear. She had showered and applied a liberal amount of sunscreen this morning, her freckles already starting to peek out from her fair complexion. She had originally planned on jeans, boots, and a T-shirt, but after meeting Tyler and knowing she'd see her again, she decided that outfit was too scruffy. She'd brought some good clothes for her time off, but those were too good for shoveling poo and cleaning kennels.

"Jesus, Cora. It's just clothes," she told herself. "She's not going to be paying any attention to you, so it doesn't matter. You probably won't even see her. She's the owner of the largest rescue kennel in the country, for God's sake." She pulled on her best worn jeans and a blue T-shirt, grabbed her socks and boots, and went to make some breakfast.

Cora's place on the beach was a two-bedroom bungalow. With the sand right off the back patio and within fifty yards of the crystal-clear water, it was almost like she had her own private beach. It would be the perfect place to unwind.

She pulled into the parking lot of Haven and instinctively started looking for Tyler's car. "You idiot. You have no idea what she drives," she told herself. However, Cora was curious, and as she drove through the parking lot she kept wondering, was that blue truck hers? How about the sleek Mercedes? Or what about that big white van? That looked like it could hold some traps and gear. And it had the Haven logo on the door. At least she knew it belonged to the rescue, but not if Tyler drove it back and forth every day. Good God. She felt like a teenager.

She greeted a few familiar faces and met several more people. Like yesterday, it surprised her how quickly she connected with everyone. Maybe it was because she was completely out of her normal element, where no one knew her or expected anything from her other than to do a good job at whatever they assigned her. Talk about freeing.

Cora signed in on the volunteer register next to her assignment for the day. She would be paired with someone named Samuel for outside play time. She didn't see Tyler's name on the list, but why would she? She was the owner and could do whatever she wanted.

Samuel was a sixty-something African American, retired stockbroker from New York. After they reviewed the case file on the four dogs that would be in the play yard together, he gave her a few basic instructions. If not for the name tags on the gates to their kennels, Cora would hardly recognize any of the dogs, their current condition almost completely opposite from their intake photo in their file. They all had recent baths, grooming, haircuts, and freshly trimmed nails. Their coats gleamed, and their tails wagged as Cora approached their kennels.

Cora chatted with Samuel about the latest political campaign, the 4th of July holiday in the US, and their mutual love of all things baseball. Samuel was a huge Mets fan and could recite just about any fact on any member of the team for the past fifteen years. Cora, on the other hand, knew almost as much about her beloved home team, the Arizona Diamondbacks. Samuel talked about why he chose to retire in Jamaica, and Cora told him she had at least another thirty years of working before she hung up her business clothes.

"God, that sounds like forever. I'm not even halfway there," she said, suddenly wishing it were tomorrow.

"Got any kids?" Samuel asked.

"No," Cora replied, surprised at the quick change of subject.

"Well, it's just like kids. Time goes by so fast, and before you know it..." He snapped his fingers so loud one of the dogs looked their way. "Sorry, Rocket," he said to the jumpy Great Dane. "What was I saying? Oh, yeah. Before you know it, the years have flown by, and it's time to go."

"Guess I'd better start putting more money away so I can retire in a beautiful place like this." Cora warmed to that idea.

"Are you married?" Samuel asked after mentioning his wife.

"No."

"Any prospects?"

"Are you applying for the role?" Cora really liked Samuel. He had a great sense of humor and, so far, was a really nice guy.

"No. Frankie would skin me alive and feed me to the fish before I even got home. Just making conversation, that's all. Frankie says I talk too much."

"Is that why you're here? So she can get some peace and quiet?" Cora found that she liked to tease him.

"Have you been talking to her? That's exactly what she says."

They were laughing when Cora saw a shadow from someone behind them. She turned to see Tyler staring at her with a peculiar expression.

"What's up, Boss?" Samuel asked.

Tyler jumped. Samuel's question had shaken her out of her almost-trance watching Cora. She'd spent most of the night dreaming of a petite, red-haired woman with eyes the color of a clear, blue sky. She'd arrived earlier than usual this morning under the pretext of checking on Agua, when in fact she didn't want to miss seeing Cora again.

"Hey, Samuel. How are you today?" she asked, approaching them. Her gaze kept drifting to Cora, and she forced it back on Samuel to listen to his answer.

"Have you met Cora?" he asked.

"Yes. We ran into each other yesterday."

Cora blushed, and Tyler thought it was cute.

"How are you, Cora?"

"I'm well, thanks. I meant to thank you yesterday for having me here."

"Well, I wasn't on my best welcoming behavior," Tyler admitted. Cora flushed again. "Please forgive me. You're here for a few weeks?" Cora had said that yesterday, but Tyler wanted to keep the conversation going. She also wanted to ask other things, but Samuel was a good safety net.

"Actually, for a month. That is, if you can stand me that long."

"That depends. If you're really good, maybe I'll ask you to stay forever."

Tyler's heartbeat raced at the words that came out of her mouth. She had no idea where they came from, but for some scary reason they sounded right.

"I don't think my boss would agree, but it's a nice thought."

"Samuel, Cora works for Bradbury Construction."

"Oh my God, Cora," Samuel said, jumping up and giving Cora a big hug. "We've been needing new kennels for months, and we just couldn't scrape up the money. Just when we thought we were about to get started, something else happened, and the money had to go there."

"Samuel is one of our long-time volunteers. He's been with us for, what, Samuel, six years?"

He nodded. "I remember digging up a parking lot by hand to make this." He gestured toward the play area.

"And look at us now. Beautiful day, four happy dogs playing in the water. How is your beautiful wife?"

"Beautiful as ever. I heard you got yourself into some trouble yesterday." Samuel turned toward Cora. "Tyler is famous for getting into tight spots while rescuing an animal."

"Hey. I get out of them, so no harm, no foul, as you Americans say."

Cora laughed and Tyler's pulse raced again, making her suddenly warm all over. She felt Cora's eyes on her as she talked.

"Well, I'll let you to get back to it. Gotta watch out for the boss. She can be a real pain."

"No. You're just a plain pussycat, and you know it," Samuel said.

Tyler returned her attention to Cora.

"Come by my office sometime, and I'll show you the plans. We break ground on Wednesday." Tyler wished she were asking Cora to dinner instead.

"Sure. I'll swing by later."

"I look forward to it." Tyler couldn't have been more truthful. She smiled as she headed back inside.

Chapter Seven

"Don't go there, Tyler," Evelyn warned her, standing by the rear door as Tyler went back inside.

"What? Where?" Tyler knew the exact location Evelyn was talking about, but she needed a moment to think.

"You know what I'm talking about. Don't do it."

"Not that I'm admitting to anything, but what exactly do you think I'm going to do?"

"Mix business and pleasure."

"That's such a stupid phrase. That's one of your American sayings, isn't it?"

"It's just as applicable as getting caught with your hand in the cookie jar."

"Even worse." Tyler immediately thought of what it would be like to have her hands on Cora. She started to sweat. What was wrong with her? She was acting like she'd never seen a beautiful woman before.

What was it about Cora that gave her the tingles all over? Sure, she was attractive and obviously smart, if she worked for Bradbury Construction. Was it because she was American? She met beautiful Americans all the time, even lesbians, but she'd never had a reaction like this. Was it because Cora was so petite Tyler instinctively felt like she needed to protect her? That was ridiculous. Tyler had the impression that Cora could definitely take care of herself. Maybe her near-death experience had rattled her more than she thought.

"Evelyn, I'm not having this conversation with you about it here," Tyler said, brushing off Evelyn's concern. Nothing was going to happen.

"Then we'll talk about it over dinner Friday. Six thirty, my place. Now get to work. I know you have some invoices on your desk you need to sign."

Effectively dismissed, Tyler couldn't help but smile. Haven and her life would be so much more scattered and chaotic if not for Evelyn.

A few hours later, a knock on her door interrupted Tyler from going through the mail that had just arrived. Cora was standing in her doorway.

"You said you'd show me the plans for the new kennels. Is this a good time?"

God, Cora was cute in her jeans and boots. She had a visor on her head and a clunky watch.

"Sure. Please come in and save me from this endless mound of paperwork." Tyler motioned for Cora to sit.

"The drudge of the existence of anyone in charge of anything," Cora said, grinning.

Tyler's stomach flipflopped. She lost focus. Their eyes met and held, and Tyler thought she would gladly drown in Cora's. They sparkled then grew dark. Tyler almost jumped out of her skin when she recognized desire looking right at her. Her mouth went dry, and it was hard to breathe.

"Are you okay?" Cora asked.

"Oh yeah, yeah—the plans," Tyler said abruptly, the heat on her face now caused by embarrassment.

"They're in the conference room." Tyler stood and came around the desk. "No room for them in here," she said, suddenly embarrassed by the mess in her office. "Follow me."

Tyler led Cora down the narrow hallway until they came to a door that had a dime-store plaque that read *Conference Room* glued at just about eye level. Tyler wasn't sure exactly what condition the conference room would be in, so she hesitated before opening the door. It was more than just a meeting room. It was a break room, lunchroom, and, with the portable cot stored in the closet, sometimes a bedroom. She breathed a sigh of relief when she saw that it was fairly clean. She didn't see any old lunch wrappers or half-empty coffee cups. The plans for the new kennels still lay in the center of the large table where she'd left them a few days ago. The room was dark, so she opened the blinds to allow the natural sunlight in.

"Here they are," she said, walking to the opposite side of the table.

The drawings were not the technical drawings needed to actually build the kennels. The construction firm had those, but the one she had access to did show the specific dimensions, elevation, and other key characteristics.

"I don't want to insult you by asking if you know how to read blueprints," Tyler said. "But you do work for a construction company."

"I'm in charge of purchasing," Cora replied, like that answered Tyler's question.

"Is that a yes or a no?" Tyler asked, still uncertain.

"That's a yes. Thanks for asking, though. A lot of people just naturally assume I don't."

"Because you're a woman?"

"Yes, that, and they think because I'm five feet tall, I'm twelve years old."

Tyler's eyes acted like they had a mind of their own as she looked Cora up and down, finally settling on her eyes.

"You don't look twelve to me." Tyler's voice was husky.

"Well, you're one of the few who don't think I do," Cora said, and Tyler wasn't sure Cora had caught her meaning. Cora pointed to something on the drawing.

Tyler proceeded to give an overview of the plans, and Cora asked more questions. When Cora stepped closer and leaned toward her to point at a specific area on the drawings, Tyler caught a whiff of her perfume. It was the same enticing scent she'd detected yesterday when Cora was on top of her. Desire shot through Tyler, settling between her legs. Cora was standing close enough that she could kiss her if she leaned in just a little. Cora stepped back, and Tyler wasn't sure if she was thankful for her sake or Cora's.

"It looks like it's going to be an awesome addition," Cora commented. "Where exactly is it going? On the side by the playground?"

"No. By the intake area."

Cora frowned and tilted her head. "I don't think I've been over there yet."

"Well, come on, then. I'll show you."

Cora eagerly followed Tyler through the building and out the door on the other side of the intake room. After standing so close to Tyler, she definitely needed some fresh air. Her enticing scent took Cora immediately back to yesterday. As she trailed Tyler out the door, Cora had a great opportunity to look at her ass, and a very fine one it was. She had had a hard time falling asleep last night, her thoughts centered around Tyler and how she was going to get through the next four weeks. Describing Tyler to Jenny hadn't helped, and thoughts of her kept Cora awake till well after midnight.

The sun was bright as she stepped outside, and Cora slid her sunglasses off her head and onto her face.

"How long have you worked for Bradbury Construction?" Tyler asked.

"About six years."

"Do you have experience in construction?"

"Only working on my own house." With a few pointers from Addison, her boss, Cora had been able to remodel her bathrooms and install a new kitchen sink, faucet, and dishwasher. She'd hobbled around for a week after spending four days laying new flooring.

"What kind of things have you done?"

Cora proceeded to give her the highlights of her remodel projects while sidestepping puddles left over from last night's rain.

"Sounds like you're pretty handy around the house."

For some odd reason the compliment made Cora feel like she'd earned Tyler's approval. But that was ridiculous. Tyler knew nothing about her, and most important, Cora didn't need anyone's approval for how she lived her life.

"I like to give things a try first. If I can't figure something out, then I call for help. YouTube has saved me thousands of dollars on installation labor fees."

"Thanks to Bradbury Construction's generosity, we contracted out the entire construction of the new kennels and yard so, unfortunately, no work for you there. And this is where they will be."

They'd stopped on the west side of the facility, or at least Cora thought it was the west, based on the position of the sun in the afternoon sky. The area had been leveled, and knee-high stakes with bright-pink flags tied at the top blowing in the breeze indicated where the building would be.

Cora studied Tyler's profile as she pointed out the markings indicating where the kennels would end and the new play yard would begin. Her skin was smooth, with only a few lines around her eyes that betrayed her age. Cora knew from her due diligence that Tyler was in her late thirties, had never been married, and wrote software code for a large technology company to pay the bills.

"Even after this, you have plenty of space to expand even more," Cora commented.

"That's the great thing about being in an industrial park. No neighbors to complain about barking dogs or vehicles coming and going at all hours of the night and weekends."

"When do you do your real job?"

Tyler turned and looked at her. "You certainly do your research," she said with a slight smile.

Cora didn't reply. It was pretty obvious.

"I'm lucky," Tyler said as they started back toward the shelter. "I'm more project-based, and as long as I turn out what they need when it's needed, I can work just about whenever I want."

"That's a pretty good gig. No time clock to punch in and out every day."

Tyler stopped and frowned. "Punch in and out?"

"That's what it's called when an employee starts and stops work," Cora explained. Some things didn't translate well in other countries. "It goes back to when workers had to insert a card with their name on it into a machine that stamped the time on the card. The payroll clerk would look at the start and end time to determine how long the employee worked and how much to pay them."

Tyler nodded her understanding and started walking again. "Right, no punch in and out."

Cora opened the door, and a blast of cool air hit them.

"Oh, wow, that feels good," Tyler said. "Sometimes you don't realize how hot it is until you go back inside."

Cora didn't answer. She was too busy thinking how good it had felt to share Tyler's excitement for the work that was about to begin.

Evelyn, the shelter manager, stuck her head out of a room. "Tyler, can I see you for a minute?"

"Speaking of punching out, my shift is over," Cora said. "See you tomorrow."

CHAPTER EIGHT

"You're spending quite a bit of time with our new volunteer, Cora."

Three days later, Tyler sat opposite Evelyn at her kitchen table, their plates full of burgers and potato chips. A can of ice-cold beer stood in front of Tyler, a Coke for Evelyn.

Tyler knew where this conversation was headed, and the best defense is a strong offense. "Not any more than any other volunteer when we happen to run into each other."

Evelyn laughed. "You are so full of bullshit," she said, shaking her head. "Do you even realize who you're talking to? I was a drill sergeant for over twenty years, and I can smell fear from a hundred yards, or meters, as you call it here."

"What do you mean fear? I didn't say anything about being afraid," Tyler said while she scrambled for some other response.

"Are you afraid I'm going to rake you over the coals for spending time with her?"

"Rake over the coals?"

Evelyn sighed. "You may have a beautiful country, but you, my dear, need to brush up on your American slang," Evelyn said. "It means give you a hard time or scold you for something you did."

"No. I am not afraid you are going to rake me over the hot coals," Tyler said. Evelyn had no trouble saying what was on her mind or voicing her opinion, and Tyler knew it was coming.

"Well, you should be, because you're asking for trouble with her."

Tyler swallowed a bit of her burger and took a drink. "Why? What's wrong with her?"

"Nothing's wrong with her, as far as I can tell."

"So, what's the problem?"

"She works for the company that gave you half a million dollars."

"So?"

"So?" Evelyn asked. "So, it doesn't look good when you sleep with the woman that works for the company that gave you that much money."

"I'm sorry," Tyler said, sitting back in her chair. "I'm not understanding."

Evelyn wiped her mouth and returned her napkin to her lap. "People might think you slept with her to get the money or because you got it."

"But I haven't slept with her."

"But you will, and people will look at you differently. And Cora too."

"Thanks for the vote of confidence, but why Cora?"

"Because they will think she's sleeping with you because you're part of the gift of the money."

"But it's not."

"It doesn't matter."

"But I'm not sleeping with her," Tyler said. She didn't think it was anyone's business who was having sex with whom.

"People will think you are."

"I cannot control what people think," Tyler said, getting angry at this circular conversation.

"No, you can't, but you can control what they see that might bring them to that conclusion."

"And are they thinking that?" Evelyn had her ear to the ground in all things at the shelter. Sometimes Tyler thought she knew more of what was going on than the actual people involved.

"No, but if you two carry on like you've been for much longer, they will."

"Carry on?"

"Act like you did. You two can't keep your eyes off each other. Even I'm starting to get embarrassed."

"Cora can't keep her eyes off me?" Tyler asked, her body signaling that it liked that idea. She'd caught Cora looking at her on a few occasions, but nothing to the extent Evelyn was describing. That was more than a little interesting…and encouraging.

"Don't act like you don't know what I'm talking about. Women buzz around you all the time, and you know exactly how to reel them in."

"Jeez, Evelyn. I'm not sure if that's a compliment or an insult."

"It's envy," Evelyn said, then burst out laughing. "If I had what you have at your age, I wouldn't be sitting here now telling you to be careful. And I am telling you just that."

Evelyn grew serious. "If any of your other donors even get a hint that you aren't one hundred percent ethical in handling donations, they'll dry up faster than a spinster's…"

"I get the idea, Evelyn. That's an image I do not need in my head." Tyler closed her eyes and squinted as if stopping any piece of that image from sneaking in.

"So, tell me," Evelyn said after they cleaned up their dinner and had retreated to the back deck with a couple of beers. "When are you going to sleep with her?"

CHAPTER NINE

Tyler, I'm sorry I can't go with you tonight. Fran just told me she has a school thing and that I have to watch the kids."

Tyler was in the supply room checking to see what she needed from the hardware store. She and George, another long-time volunteer, were scheduled to set a trap for a stray that was reported to be wandering around the marina.

"No problem, George. I can handle the trap. You go have fun with your kids."

"You can handle what trap?"

Tyler looked up from her clipboard to see Cora standing in the doorway. Her heart beat a little faster, as it always did when she caught sight of Cora. Evelyn had dragged her over the coals three days ago, but her warnings hadn't made a bit of difference in her reaction to Cora.

"I'm sorry I eavesdropped, but I caught just the tail end of the conversation. What trap?"

"We have a report of a stray out by the marina. George was coming with me to see if we could catch it or set a trap."

"I can help."

Tyler could almost hear Evelyn over her shoulder. The idea of spending time alone with Cora was enticing. Better yet, they'd be where no one would see them, addressing Evelyn's concern. This was a bad idea.

"We could be out late."

"Like I have anything else to do?"

"We're likely to get muddy and wet."

"I know how to take a shower."

Cora smiled, and Tyler's stomach tickled. A vivid image of Cora in the shower hit her. This was a very bad idea.

"Do you have jeans?" Tyler asked, taking advantage of the opportunity to look at Cora's legs.

"In my trunk."

"Let's go, then."

❖

"Are you married?" Tyler asked after they were on the road. Traffic was light, and Cora had a chance to see more of the island as Tyler drove down a wide highway.

"No."

"Have a significant other?"

"No."

"Anyone missing you?"

"If you mean other than my family and coworkers, no," Cora said, smiling at Tyler's not-so-subtle inquiry into her relationship status.

"I find it amazing that a woman as beautiful as you has not been scooped up and taken off the market." Tyler cast her a quick glance.

Cora flushed at the blatant compliment. "I haven't found anyone I want to spend the rest of my life with. How about you?"

"I'm not looking for someone to spend the rest of my life with. I'm not the spend-your-life-with kind of woman."

"Then what kind of woman are you?" Cora asked, feeling more brazen than she ever had. She'd been on the island barely a week, and here she was stepping out on a limb.

"I think I'm more what you would call dating material than marriage material."

"Are you one of those women who believe there are too many fish in the sea to catch just one?"

"Is that another American slang—fish in the sea? Evelyn is always using them. It's hard to keep up."

The light turned green. "As a matter of fact, it is. I suppose I should be a little more culturally sensitive while I'm here."

"Don't worry. We have our own sayings that probably make no sense to you."

They pulled into an empty parking lot, and Tyler drove to the far end. She turned off the engine and pulled out the keys.

"Okay. Here we go."

They got out of the van, and Tyler opened the back door. Inside, Cora could see different sizes of traps, numerous ropes and leashes, and a large toolbox. Tyler selected a key from the ring and unlocked the padlock on the bright-orange box. She opened the lid, reached inside, and handed Cora a flashlight, a headlamp, and a pair of gloves.

"Put these on. You'll need them."

She unlocked another box and pulled out a box of dog treats and shoved a handful of them into the pockets of her jacket. Finally, she reached back in and grasped what looked like a rifle with a funnel on the end.

"What is that?" Cora asked. She knew it wasn't a rifle. No way would Tyler shoot an animal.

"A net launcher."

"What does it do? How does it work?"

"Just like a rifle but it shoots a net that opens up and drops down on the animal. It takes a little bit of practice, but it works really well on animals you can't get close enough to leash or can't trap."

"Are we going to use it?"

"No. Too many things around it'll get caught on. It's best used out in the open."

Tyler secured the gun to the inside of the van and pulled out a long pole with what looked like a collar on the end.

"It's a catch pole," Tyler said without Cora needing to ask. "It's the safest way to catch and control an animal. It doesn't hurt them."

She wrapped a bright-green leash around her neck, locked the doors, and started walking. Cora eagerly followed.

"We had a report of a scruffy white, medium-sized dog running around in this area," Tyler said as Cora hustled to keep up. She was a woman on a mission.

"Whoever called it in said she was limping, so she's obviously hurt. Hurt dogs are frightened and scared, and they'll do one of two things—run or bite."

"Like the dog you brought in the other day?" Cora pointed to the bandage on Tyler's hand.

"Yes. It doesn't happen very often, and we don't want it to. So stay behind me and do exactly what I say, when I say it."

"Gotcha. Oh, sorry. Yes, of course." Cora hurriedly corrected her slang.

They walked around the area in what Cora recognized was a grid pattern. She stayed behind Tyler and moved as quietly and deliberately as she did. Without being told, she knew it was important to keep any noise to a minimum. Suddenly Tyler stopped, and Cora almost ran into her.

Tyler pointed to her left. Cora didn't see anything, but as her eyes adjusted and she looked a little harder, she saw what appeared to be a heap of rags in the corner between the fence and a building. Tyler slowly approached, and Cora watched, fascinated, as Tyler tried to get close enough to the dog to put the loop around its neck.

"That's not going to work," Tyler said after the dog had fled at least a dozen times. "We'll set up a trap and then wait and see what we get. I think she'll come in. By the way she ate the treats, she's starving and won't be able to resist the food inside it."

Cora helped Tyler maneuver the wire cage into place. It was about the size of a footlocker and looked scary.

Tyler must have read her mind because she said, "It's perfectly safe and humane. A spring-loaded hinge closes the door once the animal is safely inside."

Tyler opened a can of cat food and dumped it out on the trigger pad.

"Cat food?"

"Actually, any food will do since these animals are so hungry. This is the easiest to transport, and any hungry animal will smell it and come investigate.

"There. That should do it," Tyler said, backing away from the trap. She'd used a few old blankets Cora had retrieved from the van to hide the trap as much as she could. "Now we wait."

"How long will it take?" Cora asked as she followed Tyler across the lot in the opposite direction of the van.

"It depends. If she's not too frightened, it might be a few hours. If she's really scared, she might not come back at all. She might think this place isn't safe anymore. But I think she'll be back."

Tyler spread out a blanket next to a dumpster that must have been recently emptied because it didn't reek of old garbage.

"Why do you say that?" Cora asked, sitting down beside her.

"Just a hunch. It might be a while, though. We'll give it a few hours, then call it a night if she's not back yet. I think Samuel lives out this way. I'll have him check it on his way in in the morning."

They talked in whispers for a few more minutes, and then they both were quiet. Cora wondered what drove Tyler to give so much of her time and money to help these animals. What she did was admirable, to say the least.

An hour later, they were lying on their stomach watching the trap when Tyler whispered barely loud enough for Cora to hear.

"There she is." Tyler had a pair of binoculars up to her eyes.

"Where?" Cora asked, keeping her voice low.

"Over by the garbage cans. Damn," Tyler said, an edge in her voice.

"What?"

"I think she has a broken leg. Take a look." Tyler handed Cora the binoculars. The strap was wrapped around her neck, and when Cora pulled them to her face, Tyler came with them.

"Oh, sorry," Cora said, then stopped. Tyler's face was inches from hers, and she felt her breath on her cheek. Cora's pulse skyrocketed at the look in Tyler's eyes when they went to her lips. Tyler inadvertently licked hers, and Cora's breath hitched. Cora knew Tyler was going to kiss her. She wanted Tyler to kiss her. She needed to feel how soft her lips were, the tentative touch of her tongue, the mingling of their breath. Tyler leaned in.

"We got her!" Tyler said an instant before their lips met. Cora was a little slower on the uptake, her head foggy with desire.

"What?"

"I heard the trap close. We got her," Tyler repeated, sitting up and pulling the binoculars from around her neck. "Come on."

Cora accepted Tyler's outstretched hand, and her knees were a little weak when she stood. Whether it was from being in the same position for too long or because Tyler had almost kissed her, she wasn't sure. Either way, both situations were over, and she hurried to catch up.

"That was amazing," Cora commented after they had secured the dog and trap inside the van. "You were right. She did come back."

"She was just scared and needed someone with a little bit of patience. After a while she learned we weren't here to hurt her, and the rest was pretty easy."

"Not all your rescues are that easy."

"No. We were lucky this time. Some of them are difficult."

When they got back into the van, Tyler said, "We'll take her back to Haven, have her leg looked at, and see what we can do for her."

"She definitely needs a bath and a haircut," Cora commented, waving her hand in front of her face. "She stinks."

"You're right. A dog's entire demeanor can change after it's spent some time at the groomer. Getting all that excess matted hair off will make a big difference."

"What's been your most difficult rescue?"

As they drove back to the shelter, Tyler regaled Cora with sometimes funny, sometimes sad stories of some of her rescues. Cora reacted every time Tyler smiled and chuckled or used her hands to describe something. The passing streetlights lit up Tyler's face, her eyes sparkling. Before too long they were back at the shelter, and

Tyler handed over the pup to a couple of the volunteers. She turned to Cora.

"Let's go get cleaned up. We're a mess."

Cora looked down at her jeans and boots. They were caked with mud, though she didn't remember how they got that way. She had been so focused on Tyler and what she was doing, she hadn't noticed whatever they'd gotten into. In addition to being filthy, Cora detected an odor that was not pleasant.

"Great idea. I'm starting to stink."

Cora followed Tyler into her office, where she reached into a file cabinet and pulled out a pair of scrub pants. She tossed them to Cora. "Here. These should fit you."

Tyler pulled out a second pair, and before Cora knew what was happening, Tyler had kicked off her boots and unzipped her pants. When she slid them down her legs, Cora's eyes followed them until they hit the floor. Cora thought she'd stopped breathing because she was suddenly light-headed, and her mouth was dry. She knew she was staring, but she really couldn't do anything to stop herself.

"Oh. I'm sorry, Cora, if I embarrassed you. I forget. Everybody is used to seeing me look like this." Tyler gestured toward her soiled clothes. "I usually come in here and put on something clean. This really isn't my underwear. I think you Americans call them booty shorts."

Cora couldn't think. All she could see was bare long legs in front of her. Her mouth dropped open at the booty-short comment, and she realized she was standing here embarrassing herself.

Pull it together, Cora. It's not like you've never seen a pair of legs before.

"No. That's okay." Cora was stuttering foolishly. When she was finally able to look at Tyler, fire blazed in her eyes. Tyler obviously knew exactly what she'd been thinking. She wanted to run her hands up and down the dark legs, followed by her lips. Straddle those firm thighs and rock against them until she couldn't stand it anymore. Feel Tyler's legs wrapped around her waist as her fingers slid inside Tyler. Oh, my God, she was in big, big trouble here.

Cora untied her boots and pulled off her soiled jeans. She

hesitated for a second, wondering what underwear she was wearing. They weren't booty shorts, but her boxer briefs were somewhat modest. She wore less at the beach. Why was she embarrassed? She put one foot, then the other in the blue scrubs, pulled them up, and tied them at the waist before looking back to Tyler. Tyler had the same expression on her face that Cora must've had moments ago. Desire shot through Cora. Tyler wanted her, plain and simple. Cora wanted Tyler, plain and simple. But there was nothing plain and simple about it. If they kept this up, Cora's head would explode.

Tyler stepped forward but stopped when one of the veterinarians came into the room.

"She has a broken leg. Looks like a car might've hit her."

The vet's arrival was probably the only thing that stopped them from falling to the couch and fucking each other senseless. Cora needed to get a grip, and she needed to get it fast. She might have hooked up with a total stranger in an airport lounge, but not only was she representing her company, she was going to be here for a few more weeks and see Tyler practically every day. And everyone else, for that matter. She didn't want to be the subject of gossip. Her stomach twisted as she realized she didn't want to be another of Tyler's conquests. The woman had admitted she was not marriage material.

Where in the hell did that come from? Cora could care less if Tyler was marriage material. She wasn't planning to marry her.

Cora's stomach chose that time to growl, loudly. Both Tyler and the vet looked at her, and Tyler started laughing.

"Sorry. I missed lunch," Cora said, slightly embarrassed. "I think I'll head out."

Tyler opened her mouth and looked like she was going to say something. Was she going to invite her to dinner? Maybe dessert. Before she gave in and let Tyler ask, she said good night and hurried out the door.

CHAPTER TEN

For the next week, Cora seemed to be everywhere Tyler was. Was it fate, or did Cora maneuver her way into Tyler's sight line? Tyler didn't care. She enjoyed spending time with her and looked forward to it every day. They laughed about the first meeting as they hosed out the kennels and shared other embarrassing moments in their lives. They took turns tossing balls to the dogs in the play area, and Cora had accompanied Tyler on several other rescues. Their almost-kiss never presented an opportunity to be continued, and Tyler was growing frustrated. It had been several weeks since she'd had a good orgasm by someone other than herself. She had gone out the past several evenings, but no one caught her attention. Several women had approached her, but she was uncharacteristically not interested.

She and Gabrielle had eaten dinner together the night before, and her sister had been as subtle as always.

"Well, have you slept with her yet? How was she? Did she make your eyes roll back in your head?"

They had just toasted to their sisters' night out. "Jeez, Gabrielle. I told you I'm not going there."

"But you want to."

"How do you know these things?" Tyler asked. "You have never met the woman or seen us together."

"I hear it in your voice, and I can see it in your eyes, Tyler."

"You're making that up. You're just saying that to get me to admit I want to sleep with her."

"See, you do admit it," Gabrielle said proudly.

"I did no such thing." But I have thought about it constantly. Tyler flushed, remembering the very vivid dream she'd had last night.

"You dirty dog, you have slept with her," Gabrielle said.

"No. I have not. I was just remembering a dream about her."

"Was it hot? Was she good? Please tell me everything. I have a three-year-old at home, and Francois and I can barely say good night before we crash. We haven't had sex in weeks."

"Lalalala," Tyler said, putting her hands over her ears. *"I do not need to hear about your sex life."*

"I have no sex life. That's the problem. I need to live my life through you."

"You know I don't kiss and tell, and I definitely haven't kissed Cora, so there's nothing to tell." Tyler had to think for a moment if that sentence even made sense.

"But you want to." Gabrielle was not going to give up. She was like one of her rescued dogs with a meaty bone.

"All right. Yes. I want to."

"So, do it."

"Gabrielle, I am not having this discussion with you again. We've been through this many times, and nothing has changed." Except for the fact that Cora is driving me crazy.

"You do need to get laid. You're no fun." Gabrielle fake-pouted.

"Ditto right back at you. Show me the latest pics of my handsome nephew so you can go home and get laid. You've been a bit of a crab lately."

"Hey, Tyler?"

Samuel jolted her back from remembering her dinner conversation.

"We're going out for pizza. Do you want to come?"

"No, thanks. I've got some work to do." She had mountains of it for her paying job, and she'd be up half the night finishing it.

"If you change your mind, we're taking Cora to Harry's."

Tyler's ears perked up at Cora's name and her favorite pizza joint. There was nothing wrong with enjoying some good food and a few beers with her staff, was there? Wasn't that building loyalty and employee engagement? What a crock, she thought, using one of Evelyn's American phrases. She wanted to spend more time with Cora.

"Why didn't you say that in the first place," Tyler said, trying to keep the excitement out of her voice. "I'm in. Let me clear up a few things, and I'll meet you there."

Harry's was a small hole-in-the-wall joint off the tourist path. It had the best pizza on the island and the coldest beer in the Caribbean, both of which were her favorites.

Samuel and several others were sitting at a booth in the rear of the small room. They waved her over, and the only open seat was next to Cora. She slid into the booth and stopped just short of their legs touching.

"It's about time you got here. We're already two beers ahead of you. You better drink fast to catch up," Michael stated, filling a mug and sliding it in front of Tyler.

When she reached for it, her forearm brushed against Cora's, and a jolt of warm current spread through her. Cora didn't move away.

"We were talking about how fast the new kennels were going up. Cora was telling us about one of the contractors that came to do some work on her house." Samuel filled Tyler in and turned to Cora. "Go on."

As Cora spoke, Tyler didn't know whether to focus on the way she used her hands to talk, the melodic sound of her voice, or the feel of Cora's thigh pressing against hers when she moved. All were fabulous and all equally distracting. When everyone around the table laughed, Tyler joined in but wasn't sure what she was laughing about. Three large pizzas were placed in the table in front of them, and there was a lull in the conversation while everyone had their first few bites.

"Oh, my," Cora said after swallowing her first one.

Cora was practically purring beside her, and Tyler almost choked on the bite she was trying to swallow.

"You were right," Cora said, clearly in awe. "This is absolutely delicious."

Conversation picked back up again, and no one seemed to notice that Tyler hadn't said much. She was too busy trying to keep from pressing her thigh into Cora's. Tyler wasn't sure if the contact was accidental or deliberate. All she knew was that she was hot all over, and it was not a warm night.

The topic shifted to rescue missions as Cora told about one specific one she'd been on with Tyler. Tyler remembered all too well the time they'd spent together in the middle of nowhere with the full moon high overhead. She had wanted to kiss Cora so bad she ached. She knew Cora wouldn't push her away, but the voice in the back of her head said to keep their relationship strictly professional.

She argued with herself as if she had a devil on one shoulder and an angel on the other, each trying to convince her of their position. Tyler was more confused by her indecisiveness than anything else. Never before had she hesitated when all the signals coming her way were blinking green.

Devil: *"What would it hurt?"*
Angel: *"Don't do it."*
Devil: *"Don't listen to her. She is too cautious and doesn't know how to have a little fun."*
Angel: *"I'm thinking with my head and not other parts of my body, and I do know how to have fun."*
Devil: *"She is all over you."*
Angel: *"The booth is small and crowded."*
Devil: *"She keeps leaning into you."*
Angel: *"The booth is small and crowded."*
Devil: *"How many more times does she have to press her leg against yours for you to reply to her message?"*
Angel: *"The booth is small and crowded."*

Devil: *"She's perfect. She doesn't live here, won't make demands, and will leave the country in a few weeks. How much more perfect is that?"*

Angel: *"Don't do it. You know better than that, Tyler."*

Devil: *"I bet she's awesome in bed."*

Angel: *"Don't do it, Tyler."*

Devil: *"I bet she can rock your world and make you see stars."*

Angel: *"Rocking and stars are not all they're cracked up to be with this complication."*

Devil: *"If she touches your leg and you don't jump her, you're hopeless."*

Angel: *"Don't do it, Tyler."*

Tyler was getting whiplash from the back-and-forth of her conscience. What in the hell was going on with her lately? She couldn't focus on her paid work, had been totally distracted during the trappings, and her dreams were filled with images of Cora.

"What do you think, Tyler?" Michael asked.

"I'm sorry. What?"

"Hello? We've been talking to you. Where have you been?"

"Sorry. You caught me…" Cora pressed her leg against Tyler's and her voice cracked, "daydreaming."

"Whatever you were dreaming of had all your attention. You didn't even hear us."

Tyler flushed with embarrassment. "Sorry. I guess I'm distracted thinking about the shelter and the construction." Tyler was lying, using the first excuse that came to mind. It wasn't too far from the truth. Cora was at the shelter, and Cora's company had financed the new kennels.

"Anything I can help with?" Cora asked, placing her hand on Tyler's thigh. "I'm here to do anything you need."

"Holy shit, Tyler. You have got to do something. Now!" Devil said joyously. She could practically feel her jumping up and down on her shoulder.

"No, thanks. I think I'll just head home. I'll get the tab since I'm not much company tonight." Tyler reluctantly slid out of the booth, and the space left over loomed empty.

"Coward." Devil was disappointed.

"In that case, order us another round on your way out," Samuel said.

Everyone laughed except Cora, who was looking at her as if she were crazy. Tyler knew she must be.

CHAPTER ELEVEN

I don't know what I have to do to get her to make a move."

"Why does she need to make the move? You're a grown woman, Cora. You do it. She's obviously interested."

"You know I don't do that, Jenny." Cora had called Jenny after coming home from Harry's. She'd told her about all the body contact that had occurred between her and Tyler but to no avail. When Tyler had walked across the noisy room, Cora had hoped she would sit beside her in the booth and not pull up a chair on the end. Tyler had sat down, leaving room between them, and Cora had quickly closed it.

Whenever Tyler shifted away from her, Cora followed. She pressed her thigh or her arm against Tyler and felt the heat of her body through her clothes. Cora was acutely aware of Tyler's reaction to her advances and had been completely surprised when Tyler abruptly got up and left.

"Well, from what you've told me, Cora, if you want her, you're going to have to pull up your big-girl panties and do it."

"I don't want to pull *up* my panties. I want her to pull them down." Cora was more than a little frustrated. She had been way out of her comfort zone, and it had gotten her nowhere. So much for building confidence.

"Then you're going to have to take her hand and show her where you want it," Jenny said.

"Maybe she changed her mind. Maybe I did something to turn her off."

"Maybe she's just plain stupid," Jenny said. "Didn't you tell me she almost kissed you?"

"Yes."

"And you keep catching her looking at you?"

"Yes."

"Then she is stupid if she hasn't jumped your bones. It's been, what, over two weeks? You're running out of time. Unless you want a one-night stand on your last night or it ending up as your biggest regret, you have got to take charge."

❖

Cora was in the backyard of the halfway house playing with Spider, the dalmatian that had been rescued five weeks earlier. She had volunteered to stay a few days at the house when Jack, one of the two caretakers, had to go out of town unexpectedly for work. She thought it would be good to get away from Tyler before she made a complete fool of herself and lay down in front of her naked. She'd been seeing Tyler more and more every day, somehow finding themselves in the same room or part of the shelter several times daily. They had chatted over lunch and shared some harmless flirtation a time or two. Cora had kept it light but wanted it to be for real. Neither of them mentioned the almost-kiss.

It had been several days since her proposition to Tyler at Harry's had been shot down. Cora thought she'd made her interest clear, but maybe not. She was a little rusty. She had thought of little else while at Haven, and she was especially focused on Tyler while she lay on a beach chair near the water. She imagined Tyler in a bikini coming out of the ocean, approaching her with wanton desire and intent written all over her face. Tyler would take her hand and lead her inside and take her any way and every way she wanted. Take, hell. Cora would gladly give. She had never wanted a woman as much as she wanted Tyler, and she hadn't even slept with her yet. That usually came after the first time. Something better happen soon, or she would implode. How would she explain that?

Tyler was a very attractive woman. She had a great sense of humor, told interesting stories of animal rescues, and everyone in the shelter loved her. There was an energy in the room whenever Tyler was near, and she took it with her when she left. On more than one occasion, Cora caught Tyler looking at her with more than professional curiosity. She wondered what the locals thought about fraternization. She was a volunteer, not an employee, but that would still be frowned upon at home. Did that matter here?

Cora had just finished tossing the ball when she heard Tyler's voice behind her. She was not expecting to see her.

"You've got a pretty good arm there."

Cora warmed all over. "It's a requirement to get your lesbian card—be able to throw a ball decently." Cora stopped, shocked at what she'd just said. The heat of embarrassment ran up her neck and over her face.

Tyler's eyebrows slowly rose. "I was not aware that was a requirement. Is that a United States thing?"

Cora wished she could slide under any one of the nearby steppingstones. She had never been as bold or flirtatious, but it was as though when she was around Tyler, she became a completely different person. Jenny would be proud.

"No. Is it a requirement here in Jamaica?"

"Is that your way of asking me if I'm a lesbian?"

Cora paused a moment before answering. She could play dumb, or she could just face the question head-on.

"I think I already know the answer to that question."

Tyler's smile deepened, and she looked at Cora from the top of her dusty boots to the Nike visor on her head, lingering at all her girl parts before settling back on Cora's eyes. Judging by the fire of desire in her eyes, Tyler definitely liked what she saw.

"Let's just say I have some experience throwing a ball as well."

Cora's clit throbbed in tempo with the racing of her heart. The electricity that crackled through the air every time they were together was deafening. Cora took a step back, putting more distance between them.

"Tyler, I hate to do this, but I have to leave." Ruth, the other caretaker, came running out the back door, a harried look on her face. "My son was just in a car accident, and he's going to the hospital."

"Of course, Ruth. Go and be careful," Tyler said, shooing the distraught Ruth toward the house.

"I hope everything will be okay." Cora had just met the woman, who was warm and welcoming.

"Me too. Ruth is a wonderful woman. She's been a volunteer for years. She and her husband Jack were the first people I thought of when I was envisioning this house. They love animals and had talked about selling their home, now that all their kids were gone. It was perfect timing. They sold their place in a month and moved in here straightaway."

"How did you get this place?" Cora asked when they sat down on the patio. The sun was hot, and the shade was a nice relief.

"I'd been thinking about it for a long time. The dogs we rescue are afraid of everything. Most of them have never been someone's pet and don't know what they're supposed to do. They're shy, nervous, lack self-confidence, and don't know how to interact with people. We want to help them become a family pet, so we teach them things like making eye contact with a person, walking on a leash, and even learning how to play. The slightest unfamiliar experience can make them want to run. They may have had an unpleasant experience with something, or they have no idea what the sound is. They've never heard the dryer ding or a TV or bread popping up from the toaster. These everyday things scare them, and this house is helping change all that."

From her research, Cora knew all of this, but to hear Tyler's commitment to these animals in her voice and in the expression on her face was admirable. She told her as much.

"It's not just me. It's all the staff and volunteers and the people who have graciously donated to us. This house," Tyler spread her hands, "was purchased from the generous donations of two fabulous people who are as passionate about every animal finding a forever home as the rest of us."

Cora's admiration of Tyler jumped another few notches. The staff had shared with her many, many stories about Tyler's rescues and her level of devotion to the capture and care of unwanted animals. Her unwavering commitment to helping those that were completely helpless was inspiring. She was strong and confident, and that was just plain sexy.

Spider barked for attention, and they tossed the ball for him a few more times.

"I guess I better find someone else to come by," Tyler said. A local regulation mandated the house have two people on the grounds at all times. It didn't make any sense to Cora, but then again Jamaica was not her country.

"You could stay," Cora said, not sure if her offer would be rejected—again. Jenny had been right. If she wanted something to happen, she'd have to make it happen. She didn't want losing the opportunity to be with Tyler to be her biggest regret because she was chicken.

Tyler studied her as if trying to determine if there were other words between the lines. Before Tyler had a chance to answer, Cora stepped closer, took Tyler's face in her hands, and kissed her.

This kiss started tentative, but not for long. This kiss held promise, excitement, and potential.

Cora wrapped her arms around her neck and ran her fingers through Tyler's hair, pulling her closer. Tyler shifted, and they connected just like they had the first time they met—without the dirt and the poo.

Cora's arousal kicked up when she remembered how good it felt to be this close to Tyler. She pulled her lips away and struggled to catch her breath. Why hadn't she done this days ago? Why hadn't she done this the first day she got here?

"That's the best idea I've heard in a very long time," Tyler said before pulling Cora back in for another kiss.

CHAPTER TWELVE

Tyler closed and locked the door behind her. The dogs had been fed and watered and would come in and out the doggy door as they wished. The lights were off, but one light was shining brightly at the end of the hall. She knew it was coming from one of the bedrooms.

Tyler was uncharacteristically nervous as she walked toward the bedroom, the light her guide. Her mouth was dry, and she hoped her shaking legs could get her down the hall. She was imagining what she would see when she looked inside the bedroom Cora had chosen. Would she be naked underneath the covers? Standing beside the bed waiting for her? Sitting on the small couch Tyler knew was under the bay window?

Tyler swallowed as she stepped inside the large room. Cora wasn't in any of those places or anywhere else in the room. What the hell? Just then Tyler heard the shower door close, and her pulse kicked up more than a few beats. Cora was in the shower.

Images of warm water sliding down Cora's body were instantly replaced with Tyler's hands taking the same path. Soap was replaced with her mouth covering her curves. She pictured Cora pressed against the tile wall, her legs spread as Tyler sucked one nipple and slid her fingers into her. She imagined the feel of Cora wrapping her arms around her to keep from falling as she climaxed.

"Jesus," Tyler muttered, her breath coming in gasps.

"Tyler?"

Tyler gasped even harder, and her eyes shot open. She certainly hadn't expected Cora to be standing in the doorway draped in a towel. Her hair was piled on the top of her head in a messy bun, and Tyler had never seen anything as beautiful as Cora was right now. She wanted to discover what was underneath.

"Tyler?" Cora asked again.

"Yes?"

"Are you okay?"

"Yes."

"Do you want to join me?"

"Yes." *God, could she say anything else than a single word?*

Cora smiled, dropped the towel, and held out her hand.

Tyler's heart stopped, and she swore her mouth dropped open. Cora was exquisite.

"Tyler?"

"Yes." Yes to I hear you. Yes to I want you. Yes to anything you want.

"The water's getting cold."

Tyler finally snapped out of her stupor and shucked off her clothes, leaving them in a pile on the floor.

"Thank God I installed an extra-large water heater," she said as Cora pulled her under the water.

When the hot water finally ran out, they dried each other off. Tyler was also glad she'd sprung for the extra-soft fluffy towels. She was even happier when she thought about the high-end sheets on the bed. Cora kissed her senseless, like she had for the last twenty minutes.

"Let's do all that again." Cora's eyes were gleaming with desire. "But this time lying down."

"If you insist," Tyler replied as Cora pulled her toward the bed.

This time when stars flashed in Cora's head, she lay flat on her back, with a death grip on the sheets. Tyler was between her legs, one hand pinching a nipple, her mouth the cause of her current orgasmic bliss.

Sex in the shower had been fast and hot. It was base and carnal, and Cora wouldn't have had it any other way—at least not that time. She wanted Tyler so bad, she couldn't wait for slow and seductive. She needed her hands on Tyler, taking her to heights she'd never gone before. They'd made good use of the built-in seat and the hand-held showerhead, taking turns and, at times, simultaneously exploring each other.

But now, in the comfort of her soft bed, with the light of the moon coming through the open curtains, it was much of the same. It had started out slow, Cora running her hands over Tyler's skin, watching it flush with desire. Tyler had some ticklish spots and many others that absolutely did not make her giggle. Very quickly, Cora's long, luxurious strokes turned into almost frantic demands for "harder," "faster," and "now, now!"

Cora couldn't get enough of Tyler. It amazed her how much pleasure she received by giving it to Tyler. Touching her made her pulse race, kissing her made her heart pound, and tasting her—well, that was indescribable.

But now it was her turn, and Tyler was just as attentive.

"Turn over."

Cora barely heard Tyler through her foggy brain. Her brain cells were scattered in a million pieces.

Tyler's hands were on her, guiding her onto her stomach. Cora wasn't sure where this was going, but she trusted Tyler and relaxed. She was rewarded when Tyler's warm body covered hers.

"You are so beautiful," Tyler whispered in her ear between kisses on her neck.

Cora shivered at the sensation and the words.

"Cold?"

"Hardly."

"Good."

Tyler pushed her pussy into Cora's ass, and she instinctively rose to meet her.

"Easy," Tyler said, backing off her pressure a bit. "You keep that up, and I'll come."

Cora raised her ass to tease her. "Isn't that the point?"

"Not yet, it isn't."

"Killjoy," Cora said, laughing.

Tyler bit her neck, just a little bit of pain and a whole lot of erotic pleasure.

"You are going to regret that comment."

Tyler raised herself, and Cora instantly felt the loss. Tyler slid her hand between Cora and the sheet and found her, warm and wet.

"You have fabulous homing skills," Cora said, lifting her hips off the bed to give Tyler better access.

"You bet I do."

Cora gasped when Tyler rubbed her clit.

"Up on your knees," Tyler said, using her hands to lift her.

Cora's pulse skyrocketed as she anticipated what would come next. She didn't have to wait long.

Tyler straddled her, her pussy again grinding into Cora's ass. Cora was on her knees, her elbows on the bed, dropping her head into the perfect position to look under her and see Tyler's hand on her. The image of Tyler's fingers on her clit while she pleasured herself on Cora's ass was more than she could take. Cora exploded in an earth-shattering, indescribable orgasm.

Tyler was seconds away from coming, but she held off to watch Cora's orgasm rip through her. It was the most beautiful thing she had ever witnessed. And she knew she would never tire of watching it. Every time Cora came was similar but different. Her movements, quickened. Her breathing became short and shallow. Her skin grew hot and flushed. As if teetering on the edge, she stilled a second before she exploded. She threw her head back, arched her back, grabbed whatever was in reach, and cried out. Sometimes she uttered terms of endearment, and other times, she spilled out nasty, erotic words that took Tyler with her. Afterward, Cora's body glowed, which usually drove Tyler to more.

Cora collapsed on the bed, Tyler on top of her. She used her elbows, so all her weight wasn't pressing Cora to the bed.

"No, come back," Cora said, reaching behind her to pull Tyler back down.

They were both breathing hard, and Tyler felt Cora shudder once more beneath her.

"Okay. You're not a killjoy."

Tyler laughed and slid her hand back under Cora once again.

CHAPTER THIRTEEN

C ora? Cora?"
   Cora jolted awake. Who was calling her name?
   "Cora?" The voice sounded closer.
   "Cora? It's Ruth. Are you up?"
   "Shit," Cora whispered, then reached over and nudged Tyler. "Tyler," she whispered.
   Cora had been sitting beside her on the couch when Ruth called, asking if she could have a few days off to be with her son. Tyler had gladly told her not to worry, hung up the phone, and reached for Cora again.
   "Give me a minute, Ruth. I'm just about to jump in the shower. I'll be right out." Cora's heart was galloping. "Tyler," Cora whispered again, nudging her a little harder. Cora threw off the covers and jumped out of bed.
   "Hmm?"
   "Shh. Be quiet. Ruth is here." Cora hustled over to the bedroom door, closed it, and locked it. She had been so preoccupied with getting her hands and mouth on Tyler, she hadn't even thought about where they were and what time it was.
   Tyler sat up, the sheet falling to her lap, exposing her perfect breasts. Cora was momentarily sidetracked.
   "What is it? Is it one of the dogs?" Tyler tossed off the covers and jumped out of bed. Her complete nakedness was more than a little distracting.

"Shh. Ruth is here," she repeated urgently.

"Oh, so?"

"So? Ruth is *here*."

"Okay." Tyler drew out the word.

Cora couldn't believe Tyler was this calm.

"She can't find you in here."

"The door is locked. She won't walk in on us."

Frustrated that Tyler didn't understand, Cora spelled it out for her.

"She cannot know you spent the night here."

"She knows two people need to be here all the time and that I would probably stay. I've done it before."

"No, *here*." Cora pointed to the bed that obviously had seen a lot of action during the past few nights. Tyler finally comprehended the issue.

"You don't want Ruth to know we've been sleeping together?"

"I don't want anyone to know we've slept together," Cora said, picking up their clothes strewn around the room.

"Morning-after regrets?" Tyler asked, calmly standing by the bed and still completely naked.

Cora stopped her craziness. "It's a little late for that, don't you think? No. No regrets." She didn't have to think about that answer.

"Then what's the problem? We're consenting adults. Ruth knows I'm a lesbian. Are you afraid she'll find out you are?"

"What? No. I don't care if she finds out."

"You just care if she finds out that you slept with *me*?"

Tyler's tone was a little harsh, especially her last word.

Cora was suddenly confused. Was she not making herself clear? With what they did last night and the past three days, how could Tyler think that?

"I understand." Tyler grabbed up her clothes and started putting them on. "Go ahead and shower. I'll take care of it."

"Tyler, wait," Cora pleaded. She didn't like the way this was ending, but Tyler was halfway out the French doors on the other side of the room. She either didn't hear her or ignored her. Either way, this was not how she wanted this morning to be.

"Fuck," Cora said and hurried into the bathroom. She was about to step into the shower when she glimpsed her reflection in the mirror. She stood in front of it to get a better look.

Her lips were full, still swollen from Tyler's kisses. She touched them and remembered how sweet Tyler had tasted last night. She cupped her full breasts, her nipples sensitive when she grazed them with her thumb. She looked down her body, and the memory of Tyler looking up at her from between her legs made her flush. She practically glowed. It was amazing what a little attention and mind-blowing, toe-curling orgasms could do to your skin tone. She hurried into the shower, turning on more cold water than hot.

Tyler walked around the side of the house and into the backyard. The dogs immediately sensed her and sprang up, their tails wagging as they ran to her. She tried not to think about Cora as she cleaned and filled their water bowls and poop-scooped the yard.

She had never had an experience with a woman that was as fulfilling as it had been with Cora. The sex was off the charts, with none of the clumsy first few times with flying elbows and knees. Their bodies fit together like pieces of a puzzle, which was surprising as Cora was more than a few inches shorter than she was. I guess that matters more vertically than horizontally, she thought. She rinsed her hands the best she could with water from the hose before heading back to the house. She debated going inside or getting into her truck and just going home, but Ruth had to have seen it still parked out front. Thankfully, her keys were still in her pocket, or she'd have to knock on the door to get in. How would she explain that?

"Good morning," Ruth asked when Tyler closed the door behind her. "Coffee?"

"Good morning." Tyler considered declining the offer but then changed her mind. She hadn't done anything wrong, and she really needed a cup. "Yes. Thank you. I didn't expect you back for a few more days. How's your son?"

Tyler didn't really listen to Ruth's update on her son's health because she was too busy watching Cora come down the hall. She was dressed in a pair of shorts and a red T-shirt with the Arizona

Diamondbacks logo on the front. Her hair was wet, and she smelled wonderful as she passed Tyler to get to the coffee pot.

"How is your son, Ruth?" Cora also asked.

Tyler didn't hear the second explanation either; she was too focused on Cora's hands holding the mug.

She remembered the feel of them on her, soft and gentle, then firm and demanding. The way her fingers glided into her like they had a roadmap. The way they flicked over her clit to make her come. Tyler coughed and sputtered. She'd lost track of what she was doing, and the hot coffee had scorched her throat on its way down.

"Are you okay?" Ruth asked, handing her a napkin.

Tyler felt foolish as she wiped the coffee off her chin. "Yes, fine. It just went down the wrong way." Tyler flushed, remembering all the right ways Cora had gone down. She put her cup on the counter before it fell out of her shaking hands.

"Will you be here for the rest of the day?" Tyler asked, anxious to get out of the same air that Cora breathed. For someone who had been so summarily dismissed ten minutes ago, she was having a hard time explaining that to her body.

"Yes. I'm back. Did you stay the entire time I was gone?"

Tyler locked eyes with Cora, who was standing slightly behind Ruth. She looked afraid that Tyler was going to say yes, she had, and that Cora and she had fucked almost the entire time. Cora needed to give her some credit. Just because it was the most memorable few days and nights of her life didn't mean she was going on the morning show to talk about it.

"Yes, I did. I can't break my own rules, now can I?" Tyler asked. Cora looked more than a little relieved.

"I'll head home now. I'm glad your son is going to be all right," Tyler said, hoping that was in fact what Ruth had said. Tyler doubted she would be here if he weren't.

"I'll walk you out," Cora said, to Tyler's surprise.

"Thank you," Cora said as they walked to Tyler's truck.

"For what?" Tyler asked, angry. "For the dozens of orgasms or for not telling Ruth we fucked the entire time she was gone?"

Cora stepped back like she'd been slapped. Tyler hadn't realized she was that angry. Cora stared at her, and Tyler didn't know if she was going to blister her ass because of her rude comment or kiss her. She seriously doubted it was the latter.

Cora's eyes filled with many varied expressions, some of which Tyler recognized, but most she didn't. If eyes are the window to the soul, Tyler was getting a good look inside.

The silence between them lasted far too long, but Tyler refused to look away. She still had some dignity. If this was the way Cora wanted it, she could play by those rules. She might be a rule breaker, but not this time.

Cora finally spoke before she turned away to walk back into the house. "Yes."

Chapter Fourteen

What the fuck just happened? Cora asked herself as she walked back into the house. She heard Tyler get into her truck, but she hadn't started it yet. She felt Tyler's eyes on her, and heat spread through her as she remembered other times they had been together. When they locked eyes, when Tyler took her in the shower, when she caressed Cora's entire body with only her eyes and Cora had imagined it was her mouth on her. The way Tyler looked up at her as she feasted on her, held her gaze when she made Cora climax. The way she gazed at her as she hovered over her just before she entered her.

Cora's hands were shaking when she reached for the doorknob. Somehow, she managed to get inside and close the door, leaning against it to steady herself. It was only then that she heard Tyler start the truck and pull out of the drive. Why did she suddenly feel like she was alone on an island?

"Everything okay, Cora?" Ruth asked.

Cora forced a smile. "Sure, Ruth. Why do you ask?" Cora asked, then cringed inside at her question. Talk about opening the door to walk right through it.

"You look a little tired. Did Tyler's snoring keep you up all night? I swear she snores as bad as my husband Jack."

"How do you know Tyler snores?" Cora's heart was racing. Surely Tyler and Ruth didn't...?

"The first night we moved in, she insisted on being here, and between her and Jack, I don't think I slept a wink."

Cora smiled and exhaled at the same time. "I could only imagine what that must have been like." Cora hadn't heard Tyler snore. Then again, they hadn't done much actual sleeping over the past few days.

They had taken care of the dogs, playing and working with them inside and outside the house. It felt almost domestic, and Cora found herself imagining what it would be like living with Tyler. They shared kitchen duties and made love in every room of the house.

After one exuberant session, they lay breathless, sweat covering both of them. Cora had no idea who started it, but she knew she had come first, second, and third before she had a chance to get her hands on Tyler. She had no idea where her clothes were. Tyler chuckled.

"What?"

She pointed to the other side of the room, where two dogs were sitting patiently, obviously having watched the entire episode.

"How am I going to add sex sounds as one of the things these animals need to learn?"

Tyler had a list of typical household sights and sounds the dogs had to become accustomed to. They had spent ten minutes this afternoon popping popcorn as one of the lessons.

Cora looked to where she was pointing. "I don't think it's a problem for those two. It's your house and your training. However, I'll be happy to train any other dogs that come here. As often as it takes." Cora had kissed Tyler and rolled her over onto her back.

"Are you sure you're all right, Cora? You look flushed."

Ruth stepped close and put her hand on Cora's forehead. It must be a mother thing because her mother had done it all the time.

"I'm fine," Cora said. "Really."

"If you're sure," Ruth asked, looking her over again.

"Positive."

"All right then," Ruth said. "But I'm going to keep an eye on you. Have you eaten? I'm starved." Ruth headed toward the kitchen.

❖

Tyler drove home, her mind more on Cora than on the road in front of her. She didn't know where she stood with Cora. For a moment she'd thought their hookup was a short-term thing, but Cora's sultry response to her question completely threw her for a loop. Tyler was definitely interested in a repeat, but for the first time in her life she wasn't sure where she stood with a woman. She had to admit, being with Cora was the most powerful experience she'd ever had. She'd been with a lot of women, but none had affected her mind and body the way Cora had. She was bright, interesting, had a great sense of humor, was inquisitive, experimental, and gave just as much as she received. However, it was clear that Cora didn't want anyone to know they'd been together. She didn't understand why, but she could respect her for it.

So, what was the big deal? Like she said, they were two consenting adults. What did it matter? It was nobody's business. Tyler knew she needed to talk with Cora because she didn't want any confusion between them, since they saw each other every day. Tyler's heart skipped at a moment of panic. At least she hoped they'd continue to see each other. Cora had another week at the shelter. Panic seized Tyler when she realized that Cora would be leaving.

Tyler pulled into her driveway, her eyes gritty from not enough sleep, her skin sticky from sweat and sex. Her house was on the last block in a newer subdivision, and she'd saved diligently for years to be able to purchase it after Haven got on its feet. It was a basic model with few upgrades, and she had done her own improvements, saving her thousands of dollars. The rooms were painted in cool blues and pastels to reflect the colors of the island. She planted a small yard that didn't require too much maintenance because she never knew when she was going to be home or out chasing a stray.

She and Cora had pillow-talked about remodeling projects, sharing shortcuts and secrets to success.

On her way to the front door, she noticed the bushes could use a trim, so instead of taking a shower and a nap, Tyler washed her face, brushed her teeth, and put on her yard clothes. She'd take a long hot shower later and wipe off all the dirt and grime from the yardwork. She stopped in the kitchen before she headed out the door, her stomach rumbling. She thought of Cora. They had worked up quite an appetite last night, and not only did she need to eat, but she was also dehydrated.

After cleaning up and making a sandwich for lunch, Tyler fell asleep on the couch. She dreamed of Cora touching her, her practiced fingers knowing exactly where to go and what response they would elicit once they got there. She heard Cora's ragged voice whisper in her ear, "Fuck me." Other, equally arousing commands were uttered in the dark and in the light of day, and Tyler gladly obeyed. Cora was a demanding lover on both sides, and it was all Tyler could do to keep up.

She woke with a start, her pulse racing and her breathing coming in gasps. Rarely had she had a sex dream while taking a nap on the couch. Her phone started ringing, and caller ID showed it was Gabrielle.

"Hey there," Tyler said, sitting up and putting her feet on the solid floor.

"Were you sleeping?"

"Not after my phone started ringing," Tyler replied sarcastically. She wanted to go back to sleep and finish her dream.

"What's wrong? You never take a nap in the middle of the day."

"The only time it's a nap is if it's in the middle of the day."

"Don't be smart with me, young lady," Gabrielle fake-scolded. "Seriously, Tyler. What's going on?"

"Nothing. You constantly tell me I burn the candle at both ends, and when I try to rest, you still give me shit." That statement was the absolute truth.

"You slept with her," Gabrielle said with as much confidence as if she'd been in the same room.

"Gab…" Tyler didn't want to share what had happened between her and Cora with anyone, not even her sister with whom she shared everything. It had been more than earth-shatteringly special, and Tyler wanted to keep it all to herself.

"You can save us both some time, so don't even deny it. Just tell me."

Gabriella was a beat police officer and could get anyone to confess to anything.

"It was indescribable," Tyler said, still trying to get her head around how she had felt and still did.

"Try."

"I don't know how to explain it, Gab. It was the most amazing thing I have ever experienced. And I'm not just talking about the toe-curling sex. It was like the sun, the moon, and the stars all collided at the same time every time she touched me. I couldn't breathe or think. All I could do was feel. Every sense was alive, and about half the time I completely lost my mind."

Tyler's heart skipped a few beats when she heard the words that came out of her own mouth. She had never felt this way before. This was the kind of stuff they made sappy romance movies about. This was the kind of stuff that had always made her run very fast and very far.

"I never thought I would ever hear you talk like that about somebody," Gabrielle commented.

"I didn't either," Tyler admitted, more than a little frightened at that implication.

"What are you going to do?" Gabriella asked carefully.

"Just enjoy it," Tyler replied, surprisingly sad. "There's nothing I can do. I live here, and she lives in the US. The distance between us is not conducive to anything other than booty calls until they become too difficult to schedule and it fizzles out." Her heart plummeted.

"Ending it before it even gets started? That's not like you, Tyler. You fight for everything you want, and you almost always get it."

"This falls into the 'almost' category, then." Tyler suddenly felt the world slide out from under her feet.

"Tyler…"

"No, Gabriella. Cora leaves in ten days, and I'm just going to enjoy her and kiss her good-bye when she boards the plane."

Now only if she could convince herself of that fact.

CHAPTER FIFTEEN

H ow did you find out about us?"

"What?"

"Your donation. How did you find out about us?"

Cora was surprised at Tyler's question. Tyler had avoided her for the past several days, and she hadn't expected to start a conversation in the parking lot. Certainly not one that started like this, without even a kind hello to acknowledge what they'd done to each other and the connection they'd had while in the halfway house. How had it gone from there to here?

Still confused, Cora unlocked her rental car. "The internet is a wonderful thing." She started assembling the remaining pieces of the self-preservation wall that had been going up around her for the past few days.

"Does your company do this a lot?"

"Make donations?"

"Send people to keep an eye on the money."

Cora frowned, not sure she understood the implication of her words or why she was even saying them. She'd been here three weeks, and it was the first time the subject had come up.

"Do you think that's why I'm here? That I'd sleep with you to get close to you and report back?" Cora asked, an uncomfortable, ugly feeling starting to crawl up her neck. What was going on? Where was this coming from, she asked herself.

"Is it?"

"What are you talking about?"

"Just answer my question, Cora."

Cora's stomach dropped, and she felt sick. Was that what Tyler thought of her? That she would stoop to something so sordid as to use her body to get something? Her queasiness suddenly turned to anger. How dare she?

"We thoroughly vet the recipients before we donate anything. If we thought you were going to use our contribution for anything other than what was in your application, we would not have given you a dime, let alone the amount we did." Cora was more than a little pissed off, and she crossed her arms in front of her.

"Then why are you here for so long?"

"Because I work for a woman who believes in giving back."

"That's a big give."

"She's a big giver." Cora looked at her for a solid moment. "What is going on, Tyler?" Cora didn't even try to keep the anger out of her voice.

Tyler didn't reply, and Cora wasn't in the mood for what had turned into an inquisition.

"Look, Tyler. I have no idea what's going on here, but I'm not watching what you do and reporting back to Addison anything other than what I did on my volunteer sabbatical. What you're implying is insulting and offensive, and for some reason, I expected better from you. If you don't believe me, that's too goddamn bad." Cora was furious, and she fought to remain calm. Part of her wanted to throttle Tyler, but the other wanted to cry.

Tyler didn't reply but surveyed her up and down. What was she looking for? A lying bone? A crack in her statement? Something that would give away the real reason she was here? Well, she wasn't going to see it because it wasn't there.

"I'll honor my commitment to Haven for the next week, and I don't care what you do or what you think. I have a job to do here, and unless you throw me out, I intend to do it. Good night."

Cora slid behind the wheel and pulled her car door closed not nearly as hard as she wanted to. Not looking at Tyler again, she backed out of the space and drove out of the parking lot.

"God damn it!" Cora slammed her palms on the steering wheel and shouted into the empty car. "What the fuck, Tyler?"

❖

Tyler was scared and knew she was lashing out and being unreasonable. Her questions had come out of nowhere and, once out, took seed, and there was nothing she could do to stop them. She had worked so hard for her independence and had actually talked herself out of applying for the grant at least a dozen times. If she got the money, she'd be indebted to Bradbury in a way that was different than her arrangement with her other donors. Those people she knew, had worked alongside with for years. She understood what was in their heart. They had given freely with no expectations of anything in return other than to save animals. Bradbury Construction was a threat to her, and Cora was an extension of Bradbury. Over the past few days she had fallen for Cora in a big way, and not only could it go nowhere, but the building casting a shadow on the north lawn would be a constant, painful reminder.

"What burr is up your butt?" Evelyn demanded a few days later. She had come into Tyler's office and closed the door behind her. "You've been a crab and, at the risk of losing my job, a real bitch to everyone. And I'm getting tired of everyone asking me what's going on. The staff is walking on eggshells around you. And you look like shit."

"Well, you have quite a laundry list," Tyler replied. "First, you don't have a job. You are a volunteer. Second," Tyler held up her hand and pointed to that finger, "it's nobody's business what's going on, and if they want to know, they need to ask me. And third, even with your choice of food-related metaphors, I think I know what you're talking about, and no one needs to walk any different around me than before." Tyler was exhausted, but she didn't want to call attention to that one. Evelyn would see right through any lie she attempted to cover the fact that every time she closed her eyes she thought of Cora. What a joke. Every time she breathed, she thought of Cora.

"What did you say to Cora?" Evelyn's tone was take-no-prisoners.

"Nothing. I've barely seen her the past few days." Actually, it had been four days since she'd spoken to her in the parking lot. Not one of her finest moments. Why had she been such an ass to her? A real work project had kept her in her office, and she was secretly grateful.

"What did you do, Tyler?"

"What do you mean? I haven't done anything."

"You had to have done something."

"Why do you keep asking me that? I'm not one of your snot-nosed recruits that is going to confess to being a virgin."

"She left."

"Okay. Do you need something from her?"

"She went home. To the US," she added for finality.

Tyler dropped her coffee cup, and it bounced on the desk. She had just tightened the lid, so thankfully nothing spilled on her papers. She fought a moment of panic at the thought that Cora was gone. No longer on the island, no longer in her life every day. Gone—a very powerful four-letter word.

"She wasn't supposed to leave for another two days."

"She said something came up." Evelyn's expression hadn't changed. It was hard and unforgiving.

"Maybe it did. She is an executive in a US firm. Things come up."

"You slept with her."

Tyler wasn't sure Evelyn was making a statement or an accusation. "And you think that's the reason she left? Gee, thanks, Evelyn."

"Don't be smart with me. What did you say?"

"Why do you think I said or did anything that would cause her to run off the island?"

"Because why else would she have left so suddenly?"

"Because she doesn't live here. It was time for her to go home. Her life is not here," Tyler, said exhausted at the back-and-forth of the conversation.

"She couldn't keep her eyes off you. She lit up when you walked in the room, and you were the same way."

"Then why did she leave without saying good-bye?" Tyler's voice cracked when she realized Cora hadn't said good-bye.

"Did you give her a reason to stay?"

"What? No, of course not."

"Why not?"

"Why would I?" Tyler ran her hands through her hair. "For God's sake, Evelyn. She does not live here." Tyler separated the words to make her point. Her frustration was on overload. "What is she supposed to do? Quit her job? Uproot her life and sit in the muck for hours on a hot summer night getting eaten alive by mosquitos to *maybe* catch a stray dog?"

"What would you do if the roles were reversed?"

What would she do? Give up everything without being asked, without the slightest idea how Cora felt about her?

Cora had to have known. Every time Tyler touched her or whispered her name in the dark, she was telling her. But how would she know? Tyler hadn't realized until just this moment how much Cora meant to her. What an idiot, she thought.

Evelyn slid a piece of paper across her desk.

"What's this?" Tyler asked, picking it up.

"Cora's number. Call her."

CHAPTER SIXTEEN

B usiness or pleasure?"

"Excuse me?" Cora hadn't paid any attention to the woman sitting in the window seat.

"Going to the US," she said. "Were you here in my beautiful country on business or for pleasure?"

That was a loaded question. What had started out as business had turned very personal, very fast.

Cora had planned to work at the shelter—picking up poo, playing with the animals, giving them a bath, and whatever else they needed her to do. She was going to sit on the beach and relax, read a few books, and work on her tan. She wanted to write her fan fic and maybe even get ahead a little bit. Eating good food and drinking fruity drinks were also on the agenda. She had done most of that, but the thing that she remembered the most was the time she spent with Tyler.

They had laughed at each other's jokes and shared the household chores at the halfway house for three glorious days. They had watched the sun set and kissed under the stars. They had made out like teenagers on the couch and made love in the big, soft bed. She'd had no intention of falling for anyone, especially someone who lived thousands of miles and two time zones away. How stupid was that? And look where she was now. Sitting on a plane jammed with people heading back to her life. Back to reality. Back to long workdays sitting in a stuffy office grinding through meetings, phone calls, and more meetings because she really had no reason to go home. Nights that would be endless because Tyler wasn't sharing them with her.

Even though Cora had changed her life, was much more active and had many new and different interests, they now seemed blasé. How could one woman fill the very air you breathed even when she was nowhere near? And to think Tyler would accuse her of being there to spy on her for Bradbury. What a fool.

"I'm going home," Cora said flatly, not really answering the question.

Cora's phone exploded with messages when she turned it on after landing in Miami. She had fourteen texts, eight voice mails, and forty-two emails, but none of them were from Tyler. Disappointment hit her stomach like a rock.

Was she actually expecting Tyler to flood her voice mail with apologies and declarations of her undying love and pleas for her to come back? Not by the way she had treated Cora and the things she had said to her in the parking lot yesterday. Cora realized Tyler was right when she said she was not the marrying kind. Cora was just another broken heart left behind in a beautiful country. She turned her phone off, slid it into her pocket, and headed to her connecting flight.

End of Part II

PART III

Maui Magic

Addison and Erin

CHAPTER ONE

"Welcome aboard, ladies." Erin greeted the three women boarding her boat. Behind her mirrored sunglasses she had watched as they gathered their things from the trunk of the rental car and strolled down the dock to her boat, *Westwind*.

Her queer-dar pinged, and she mentally checked the boxes. Three women on vacation—no kids, husbands, or girlfriends. Experience had taught Erin that three lesbians traveling together were usually just friends. She'd find out soon enough.

Six hours and four very bad sunburns later, when the three women, along with her other passengers, departed *Westwind*, Erin had two phone numbers and three hundred dollars cash in tips in her pocket. She shook her head as several gingerly walked toward their cars. Did people actually think they could spend a day on the water under a cloudless sky and not get burned? Even with her native skin, Erin made sure she was always adequately covered, with a long-sleeve swim shirt and SPF 50 on any exposed skin. Her midsection and ass were a much lighter color than her arms and legs, but she wasn't going to spend her free time in the sun trying to even it out. She'd had no complaints from the women who had seen her naked—only a few giggles that she had quickly turned into sighs of pleasure.

"Sarah, your mom is here," Erin said after *Westwind* was secured for the night. Her sister-in-law's car pulled into the parking space closest to her dock.

Sarah was a natural on the water. Erin had introduced her

niece to snorkeling when she was four, and the girl had been like a fish ever since. Starting at fifteen, Sarah had worked for Erin as a deckhand for the past two years. Summers were her busiest months, with March and December coming in a close second. Sarah worked every weekend and six days a week during the summer and school breaks. It was June 1, and judging by the number of reservations on the schedule, it looked like it would be another good summer.

"See you tomorrow, Aunt E." Sarah grabbed her bag and scampered down the dock as only a seventeen-year-old without a care in the world could.

Her brother, Kamea, had met his wife Susie while in college at USC. They were an odd-looking couple—Kamea big and strong as the center on the USC football team, and Susie a petite, blond cheerleader. As corny as it sounded it was a match made in heaven, and Kamea had brought his wife back to Hawaii after graduation. Sarah was born shortly thereafter, followed by Harry, Grace, and Philip.

"Come over Sunday," Susie shouted from her car in her cheerleader voice. Or was it her mom voice? They both sounded the same. "Beer at four, burgers at six."

Erin waved her acknowledgment, and Susie drove off, her minivan blowing smoke out the backend. Kamea was a teacher, Susie a stay-at-home mom, and they were always struggling to make ends meet. But they were happy, and that was all that mattered.

Erin didn't have the words monogamy and happily-ever-after in her vocabulary. There were far too many women in the world for her to settle down with just one. Her friends had laughed when she said it would be like having the same thing for breakfast, lunch, and dinner every day. She never heard the ticking of her biological clock or felt the need to make a nest with someone. She owned her own business, had great friends, and was seriously saving for retirement. She had her pick of women, all of whom wanted no more than a vacation fling. Her life was perfect. What more did she need?

Chapter Two

Water splashed on Addison, jolting her awake. She'd fallen asleep in the chair on the beach in front of the resort. Of the eight main islands of Hawaii, Maui was her favorite. The beaches were pristine, the people generous and the views breathtaking. The soothing waves had been relaxing, and she'd quickly drifted off to sleep. Thankfully she had remembered to slather herself with sunscreen. She had rented a one-bedroom condo in a high-end complex, insisting the patio open onto the beach. She'd arrived this morning exhausted after taking a red-eye from Phoenix. The day after tomorrow she started the build.

Gathering up her bag, Addison returned to her room to shower and look for a place to eat. Rested after her nap, she donned a pair of shorts, T-shirt, flip-flops and turned her rental Jeep toward Lahaina.

Parking was always a bitch, but she found a spot in a lot at the far end of the popular shopping strip and quickly mixed in the throngs of people jockeying for a position on the narrow sidewalk. A group of teenagers almost ran her over when they exited a T-shirt shop without looking where they were going. Her destination in sight, she sidestepped several couples and more than a few families to get to an open seat at the bar of the Lahaina Pizza Company. The LPC was one of her favorite restaurants and, by the looks of the crowd, popular with many others as well.

Located on Front Street, twenty-two stairs up from the street, the restaurant was directly across from the seawall and had stunning views of the ocean and the spectacular sunset. There were no windows, only heavy canvas shades rolled up and down allowing the cool ocean breeze to blow through and keep the occasional rain out. Well-worn tabletops and chairs sat on top of a wooden floor scarred from thousands of visitors every week. Several large families had pushed tables together, and empty beer pitchers littered the tabletops, no doubt contributing to their joyous laughter. Parties of three or four occupied other tables, and a dozen sat at the bar.

Addison couldn't help but inwardly cringe when, in the reflection of the large mirror behind the bar, she saw a man and a woman at a table directly behind her. The woman wore a bridal veil, obviously just arrived for her honeymoon. Jesus, Addison thought. Why was it so hard for her to find a decent woman? Maybe she should be asking herself why she kept *failing* to find a decent woman?

Since a disastrous breakup half a dozen years earlier, Addison had been through Karen, Becky, Joanne, Mia, Jenny, and several others she chose not to remember. How could someone so successful in business be so unsuccessful in relationships? Maybe she should just stick with hookups or maybe a vacation fling. No pressure, no commitment, no drama, no disappointment.

The bartender placed her pizza on the place mat in front of her, then slid over the containers of oregano, parmesan cheese, and red pepper. After ordering another beer, Addison felt a familiar pricking between her shoulder blades. Someone was watching her. Like mothers have eyes in the back of their heads, Addison had learned long ago what it felt like to have eyes on her. From the first day she'd stepped onto the job site at fifteen, to now, she knew. She could sense it.

Under cover of biting into the piece of her pizza, Addison casually glanced at the faces reflected in the mirror in front of her. Families were laughing, couples engrossed in each other, no one seeming to notice her. She was just about to give up when her gaze stopped at a woman in a green short-sleeve shirt looking at her. She was sitting at a table, and all Addison could see was that she had short black hair and piercing dark eyes. Addison's heart skipped, and a low-voltage electrical current ran through her. The woman was definitely looking at her. Like *looking* at her. Addison tried to glance away but couldn't. It was as if the woman possessed some sort of a tractor beam and was drawing Addison in.

Heat ran up her neck, and Addison wasn't sure she was still breathing. The noisy restaurant suddenly became as quiet as midnight on a beach.

"Ma'am? Ma'am?"

The bartender moved in front of Addison, blocking the woman from her view. The disconnection was jarring.

"I'm sorry. What?" Addison scrambled to get back to the here and now.

"Are you all right? Is everything okay? You looked a little out of it for a minute."

"What? Oh, yes. Everything's fine. Thank you." Bullshit, she thought, her hand shaking as she raised her beer to her mouth.

The bartender stood there a few more minutes making small talk, but what Addison really wanted was for him to get the hell out of the way so she could see the woman again. When he finally stepped away to serve another customer, the woman was gone, her chair empty. The table she was sitting at contained evidence she hadn't been alone, but Addison had been so focused on the woman, she hadn't noticed.

She spun around on the stool, desperately looking for her. Had she just stepped out to answer a call? Gone to the bathroom? Left altogether? That thought was crushing.

"Good God, Addison. Pull it together," she said, not afraid anyone could hear what she said. The restaurant was crowded and noisy. After one long last look around, she turned back to her dinner, suddenly not very hungry.

What in the hell was that? What had just happened? It was like a scene out of one of the well-read romance novels she had on her bookshelf. Something ridiculous like, "Their eyes met across a crowded room and the world fell away. Nothing existed except each other."

"Holy shit," Addison said, this time quietly. A tremor ran through her. That was exactly what had happened.

CHAPTER THREE

I can catch an Uber if you want to go back inside."

"What?" Erin almost stumbled on the last step out of the restaurant.

"I saw you eyeing that woman at the bar. I've been your friend since before you even knew you liked girls, and I know that look."

"Jesus, Lei. You make me sound like a letch."

She and Leilani had lived down the street from each other growing up. Not only had they played together and gone to the same school, but Leilani was the captain of Erin's second boat, *Westwind II*.

Whereas Erin was on the lean side, with her hair cut short, Leilani was much heavier, her dark hair falling below her waist. She was Erin's best friend and confidante, and they'd managed to keep in touch over the years despite their families moving around the world. Erin was closer to her than to her own sister.

"No. You're usually pretty cool about it. But you were different this time. You looked at her like she was the one."

"One what?" Erin asked, hoping she sounded innocent. She knew exactly what Leilani was talking about. When she had seen the woman at the bar and their eyes had locked, it was all Erin could do to breathe. She'd also had a hard time keeping her heart from beating out of her chest, skip over to her, and curl up in her lap. Erin had no idea what had come over her and was more than a little rattled.

"Like the one that you will finally settle down with. The one that will make you want to come home to her every night. That one."

"Good God, Leilani. Have you lost your mind?" Erin replied, trying to joke her way out of a very uncomfortable feeling. "Those words make me break out in hives. You know that. You may have found your Ms. Forever, but I'm only interested in Ms. Right Now." Why did that label suddenly sound clichéd and tacky?

"You say that now, but wait. When you meet her, you won't know what hit you, and you will never look back or look around again. Trust me," Leilani said emphatically, pulling out her phone.

"Put that away. You're not taking an Uber home. I am not doing anything tonight except going home, checking the schedule for tomorrow, and going to bed. Alone," she said to the doubtful look on Leilani's face.

Erin had thought about turning around and going back upstairs. The stares she'd exchanged with the woman guaranteed she wouldn't have to sleep alone. Then she'd thought better of it. The connection, even from across the room and the reflection in the mirror, was palpable. And dangerous. She always ran from dangerous woman.

Erin had fallen in lust at first sight many, many times but never like this. As beautiful as the woman was, warning bells were clanging in her head, and Erin always paid attention to those.

Back at her house on Freebolt Street, Erin started a load of wash, grabbed a beer, and opened the back door. She'd bought the tiny house badly in need of TLC four years ago and had scraped, sanded, scrubbed, hammered, nailed, and painted on every one of her days off for the first two years. It was finally exactly how she wanted it, and a sense of pride and home filled her every time she rounded the corner and saw her little blue house.

Buoy, her springer Spaniel, scampered through her doggy door and out into the backyard. At three, she was finally past the chew-everything stage and had been the valedictorian of her class in obedience school. She dropped a grungy tennis ball at Erin's feet, sat, and looked up at her expectantly. Erin tossed the ball toward the back of the yard, and Buoy took off after it. At least twenty times they played the game, and Erin wondered who was the one actually trained.

Erin left the dog chasing a bug and went back inside to call her mom. Melia Williams was in her early sixties, a young bride of a US sailor from Michigan stationed at Pearl Harbor. She was nineteen when she married, twenty when her brother Kamea was born, and four years later came Erin and her sister a year later. Erin had asked her mother why she didn't have a traditional Hawaiian name like her siblings, and Melia had simply said she liked the name Erin, and that was that. When Melia spoke, that *was* that. Her mother's volunteer work kept her busy, but Erin called every few days just to check in. She never wanted to think about the day when she'd never hear her mother's voice again.

"Aloha, Erin." Malia greeted her warmly.

"Aloha, Mom. What are you doing?"

"Just sitting here watching your father sleep in his chair, like he does every night. He refuses to go to bed until I do."

"He's always been that way," Erin commented. "He'll never change, and I think it's sweet." Other than that scenario, Erin never thought of referring to anything as sweet unless it was dessert or that perfect spot between a woman's legs. The face of the woman from the pizza restaurant flashed through her mind.

"It's annoying," her mother said. "That's what it is." Her parents had been married for over forty years, her father spending all but the last five in the Navy. Robert Williams had taken his family all over the world, and when Erin was eighteen, she had returned to the islands. Her parents followed when her father retired.

"How is Sarah doing?"

"Better every trip. She's great with the guests, and she's a pro at small talk. Today there was a lady who was horribly sick, and by the end of the trip Sarah had her laughing. I think she gave her a fifty-dollar tip."

Her mother laughed, and Erin pictured her wide smile and inviting dark eyes.

"So how is your love life?"

"Mom." Erin hated it when her mother applied her not-so-subtle inquiry into her relationship status. It was a subject she brought up more and more lately. Thirty-six did not automatically put you into the old-maid category on the census.

"You know I'm not the type to fall in love. I missed that gene when they were handing it out."

"Phooey. It's just in the back of your closet."

Erin laughed. Her mother had a wicked sense of humor. "Everything came out of my closet when I was fifteen. You know that."

"Okay, so how is your sex life?"

"Mom!" Erin blushed when the woman at dinner flashed in her brain. She fanned herself with a piece of mail from the counter.

"I am so not having this conversation with you."

"But we share everything, ku'uipo." It was her mother's favorite term of endearment for Erin.

"True, but we don't share that."

"Maybe I need to live my life vicariously through yours."

Erin chuckled. "Wake Dad up and live your own life. I've got to go feed Buoy. She's looking at me like I haven't fed her in a week instead of just this morning."

Talking to her mother always brightened Erin's day. She had read somewhere that no matter how old you are or how successful, you always need your mother. That was definitely true with her.

The Williamses were a tight-knit family. Her sister lived in Honolulu, and Erin and her brother on Maui. Her parents had settled in Kauai. They got together every few months when life and finances lined up perfectly with the stars.

Erin was in bed by nine, her morning starting very early. She had to be up and out the door by five to have her boat ready for passengers by seven thirty.

She had purchased *Westwind*, a fifty-four-foot-long, thirty-foot-wide, double decker power catamaran twelve years ago and made her final payment last month. Eighty-four more payments and *Westwind II* would be all hers as well.

Both of her boats were rated to hold fifty-two, including the crew. She kept the maximum passengers to thirty-five, an easily manageable number. They had a slide off the top of the second deck, two heads, a multi-speaker sound system, and a barbecue. Seven days a week the *Westwind* took excited passengers on a five-hour adventure of snorkeling in one of the most popular waters on the island. She had some of the highest ratings on trip.com and several other tourist sites.

Erin had been working nonstop for months. One of her captains had taken eight weeks off when his wife had their first baby and was due back tomorrow, so she would finally have some time off. The funny thing was, she wasn't going to take any. She planned to help Susie build homes for underprivileged families. Even though it was one of the busiest times of the year, Erin needed to get away.

Susie, her sister-in-law, had been pestering her for years to join her on one of her builds, as she called them, and when Erin finally said yes, she was rewarded with a hug so tight it took her breath away. The site was less than four miles from Maui High School, and she was due on the job site the day after tomorrow. Building this house was completely unlike anything she'd ever done. She was excited to get started and wondered why she'd waited so long to volunteer. Erin had her hammer, tape measure, and gloves tucked into the designated pockets in her tool belt, and her work boots. She was ready for a new adventure.

CHAPTER FOUR

A ll right, everyone. Let's get started."
Addison quickly ended her conversation with the woman next to her and turned her attention to the front, where a short, plump woman was clapping her hands to break through the chatter of the people in the room. She'd arrived a little early and had talked with a few of the women before taking a seat in the third row. The volunteers were as varied as you would find in a shopping mall, if anyone ever went to the mall again. Some were short, others tall, and a few more, like her, carried a few more extra pounds than they'd like. Some had a nice tan, and others would need lots of sunscreen. You couldn't tell who was rich and who was struggling from day to day. But what they all had in common was their desire to help those not as fortunate as they were. The pounding of a hammer on a long, battered tabletop finally got everyone's attention.

"Ladies, and gentlemen," the woman said, acknowledging the few brave men in the room. "Thank you for volunteering for the Maui chapter of the Habitat for Humanity women's build." The room burst into applause.

"My name is CaroleAnn, and I am the project manager of this build. This is the eighth year we've been able to do this, and we couldn't do it without the generous donations of our sponsors. This year our main sponsor is Bradbury Construction." During another round of applause, Addison joined in.

"Now, let me explain what's going to happen, a few ground rules, and after our safety briefing, we'll answer any questions."

CaroleAnn proceeded to follow her stated agenda, and Addison was more than a little impressed at the safety briefing. When the question-and-answer session started, the familiar tingling began between her shoulder blades. It was the same one she'd had in the restaurant two nights ago. Addison didn't think anyone knew who she was. She'd insisted the Habitat headquarters not tell anyone. She didn't want any special treatment because of who she was or the fact that her company was financing this project.

When a woman behind her asked a question, Addison turned around under the pretext of looking at her. She took it as an opportunity to see if she could tell who was activating her sixth sense.

She had almost run out of possibilities when she locked eyes with the woman from the restaurant. For the second time, Addison found it hard to breathe, and her heart started beating way too fast. The woman was stunning in an androgenous, butch way. She was apparently Hawaiian and had intense dark eyes that bored into her.

The woman raised her eyebrows and tilted her head as if to say, "Well, hello there." It was more than a polite greeting. It was an offer. Addison's mouth suddenly was very dry, and her hands started to tremble.

She never mixed business with pleasure. She never dated anyone she worked with, no matter how tempting. The construction world was far too small, and she didn't need that complication in her life or her business. This wasn't any different, right?

The meeting adjourned, and Addison exited the room, leaving the woman's invitation unopened.

"Hey."

Addison was almost to her rental when she heard the voice behind her. It didn't take a rocket scientist to know who it was.

"Got a minute?" the woman asked.

Addison unlocked the Jeep, turned, and put the driver's door between them. Something told her she needed the reinforcement to shield her from this woman's attractiveness.

"I'm Erin Williams," the woman said and extended her hand. Addison had a choice to make, the first of many she somehow knew she'd have with her. She shook the woman's hand, and the instant they touched, a current went through her so powerful it almost knocked her back. The woman's eyes grew wide. She had clearly felt something too.

"Addison." She somehow managed to remember her name and was able to speak it.

"Is this the first time you've worked on something like this?"

Erin's voice was smooth, with just a hint of an accent. Did Hawaiians have accents? Was she even Hawaiian? Her dark skin and features looked like it, but she held a hint of something else as well. Addison suddenly felt very culturally incompetent.

"No. I've done a few things before." Like six thousand, four hundred, and seventy-two, to be exact. After her first week working with her father, Addison had kept a journal of everything she'd helped build, whether it be constructing a wall, pouring cement, painting a house, or roofing it. It didn't matter. If she helped create someone's home, she counted it. The last item in her journal was dated three years ago.

"I'm a hammer virgin," Erin said, and Addison suddenly wanted to know exactly what she could do with the right tools. She was glad it was dark so Erin couldn't see the heat run up her neck. *Jesus, where did that come from?*

"I'm sure CaroleAnn will put you on a crew that can help you. Now if you'll…" Addison needed to leave before she did something stupid like fuck this woman in the back seat. *Whoa.*

"Would you like to grab a drink, or maybe a cup of coffee?" Erin asked, taking a step closer.

Addison was grateful for the door between them. What was it about this woman that drew her like a magnet?

"I'm sorry, I can't, but…"

"I was just hoping for some pointers for tomorrow."

Erin was cute when she cocked her head and made an innocent face. About that vacation fling, a voice in Addison's head reminded her.

"Bring a hat, a good pair of gloves, and sturdy work boots."

Erin studied her for so long Addison was getting more nervous than she already was. They were the only ones left in the parking lot, and they could easily…

"Okay, I get it," Erin said, raising both hands in front of her, palms out. "I'll try again tomorrow. See you then."

Allison didn't know whether to be relieved or disappointed that Erin had given up so easily. She got in the Jeep, closed and locked the door, and sat there for a few moments before pushing the start button. "Jesus, Addison. Didn't you just tell yourself earlier to stop looking for your next failed relationship?" Shaking her head, she drove out of the parking lot.

Erin threw off the covers in frustration. She'd tossed and turned after going to bed over an hour ago. She never had trouble falling asleep, but tonight she couldn't stop thinking. About Addison.

She'd been more than a little surprised when she recognized the woman from the restaurant at the briefing tonight. She'd texted Susie, letting her know that she was running late, and crept in after the briefing started and sat in the back row. Eight rows separated her from Susie and another two from the woman.

Never good at sitting still, Erin felt her attention start to wander during the safety briefing. How difficult could it be? Don't hit your thumb with a hammer, cut your finger off with the saw, or let a wall fall on you. Not complicated.

Erin methodically went through each row, looking at each woman. She imagined what they did for a living and how long they would last on the project. For more than a few she wondered what they were like in bed. She did a double take when she recognized her. Of all the places in Maui to be on a Tuesday night, they were in the same church basement. She never would've bet on that.

The woman had looked at home in lived-in jeans, a short-sleeve shirt, and worn boots. Erin skipped right over speculating on her profession and went right between the sheets. Her imagination was quite vivid, and when she turned around, she had definitely been caught doing more than just looking. And the woman knew it. All Erin could do was nod in acknowledgment and hope her telepathic skills were working. She never had any problem with women not knowing exactly what was on her mind. When the meeting broke up, she headed straight for her, but Susie stopped her.

"I wasn't sure you were coming," Susie said, disbelief still in her voice.

"Of course I was. I told you I'd be here. I just got caught up in something. Sorry I was late, but thanks for saving me a seat. I didn't want to interrupt, so I stayed in the back."

Susie started talking, and Erin couldn't focus on what she was saying, her attention on the woman over Susie's shoulder.

"Who do you keep looking at?" Susie asked, looking around behind her.

"I think I saw someone I know," Erin fibbed. She certainly wanted to know her.

Susie turned all the way around. "Who? I know most of the regulars."

"Tall woman, dark, shoulder-length hair in a pony. Killer legs and ass in jeans."

Susie frowned then realized what Erin had said. She punched her in the arm.

"Ouch," Erin replied, rubbing just above her elbow.

"Erin Williams, don't you even think about getting lucky with someone on this project. This is serious, and someone could get hurt."

"No one will get hurt, Susie."

"That's not the hurt I mean, dummy. It's a construction site, and you have to be aware of your surroundings all the time. You can't do that and make goo-goo eyes at some girl at the same time."

"Goo-goo eyes? What are we, eight? And it's not some girl. That I'm sure of."

"You're just like your brother," Susie said, shaking her head.

"That's because he learned it all from me. And you can thank

me later. See you tomorrow." Erin dashed out the door to the parking lot to catch up with the beautiful woman.

Giving up on the conventional way to fall asleep, Erin lay on her back, imagining Addison wearing a tool belt and nothing else.

CHAPTER FIVE

Addison slung her tool belt over her shoulder, closed the door of the Jeep, and slid the key into her pocket. She pulled her hat farther down to shield her eyes from the early morning sun. As she maneuvered through the maze of cars parked haphazardly in the dirt lot, she hoped their driving habits weren't an indication of how these women worked. Exact measurements and straight cuts were critical in building anything, especially a house.

She chatted with several of the women she'd met last night while waiting for CaroleAnn to arrive. One was a baker, another a bank teller, and a mechanic and a nurse rounded out the group. Addison had simply said she worked in a real-estate office. That wasn't too far from the truth.

As much as she told herself she wouldn't, Addison looked around for Erin. For someone she'd just met, she had dreamed of her all night, and they were very vivid dreams. It had been quite some time since she woke herself up with a powerful orgasm. If Erin was half as good in real life as she was in Addison's dream, Erin's lovers were very, very lucky.

One of the women moved, and over her shoulder Addison saw Erin on the other side of the lot. She was laughing at something one of the women around her had said. Desire ran through her like warm water. Erin chose that moment to look up, and their eyes met. Heat rose up her neck as she envisioned Erin in her dream last night.

Addison was on a job site, the walls up and most of the cabinets and countertops installed. Somehow, she knew it was a Friday, and everyone had left for the weekend. She wanted to get a jump on the coming week, and she was on her knees finishing laying tile in the master bathroom.

Addison didn't hear anything, but she sensed she wasn't alone. Before she had a chance to turn around, a pair of battered work boots and paint-splattered jeans appeared in her peripheral view. She knew without looking that it was Erin. She'd felt Erin's eyes on her all day, which completely interfered with her concentration. She'd smacked her thumb with a hammer and had mis-measured twice. Addison couldn't remember the last time she'd been so rattled by having a woman nearby.

As if her eyes had a will of their own, she looked at Erin's boots and slowly moved up long legs, past the tool belt hanging low on her hips and up the tight T-shirt. From her angle, it was impossible to miss Erin's tight nipples and her chest rising and falling quickly. She continued up her neck, past luscious lips, and stopped at her eyes. Fire blazed in deep, dark pools. There was no doubt whatsoever what Erin wanted.

Addison shifted, still on her knees, and reached for Erin's belt. Never taking her eyes off Erin's, she unclipped her tool belt, the equipment rattling to the floor. She popped the first button on her jeans. Erin filled them out nicely, and Addison took her time opening each fastening.

Erin untucked her shirt and raised it, giving Addison easy access. Addison loved it when a woman took control of what she wanted. It also provided Erin an unobstructed view of what she was doing. Erin's pelvis gently rocked into Addison's fingers as she undid the final button.

Addison grabbed the waist of her jeans and slowly slid them down her legs until they pooled at the top of her boots. She slid her hands up the back of Erin's legs, her skin warm and soft under her hands.

Still looking at Erin, Addison moved closer, settling her hands *on Erin's slim hips. She wanted to rip Erin's briefs down and bury her face between her legs, but there would never be another first time to inhale her distinctive scent, to see her, to touch her. Addison forced herself to slow down.*

Dipping her fingers under the waistband of her briefs, Addison slid them over Erin's hips, each agonizing second revealing more and more of what lay beneath. Finally, the briefs joined the jeans, and Erin stood before her, her arousal in the air.

Addison cupped Erin's ass and leaned in, the first taste seconds away. She buried her face in Erin's dark hair and savored her scent. She might not have a second chance and wanted to remember this forever.

Erin spread her legs as far as she could and grabbed the frame of the doorway with each hand. Addison's breath squeezed out of her lungs at the sight of this woman before her, offering herself for Addison to take.

Addison slid her hands around and parted dark, wet lips revealing glistening pink flesh. Erin spread her legs wider, her jeans an impediment to complete freedom. Addison toyed with the idea of removing her boots and pants completely, but she preferred her this way—completely at her mercy.

Erin's breath quickened as Addison's mouth moved closer. When Addison's tongue touched her, Erin gasped and wrapped one hand behind her neck. Addison's excitement skyrocketed as Erin signaled exactly what she needed. She wondered who was actually in control here.

Addison used her tongue to explore, taste, and tease Erin until both of them were breathing fast and hard. With one hand on her ass, Addison slipped a finger into Erin's warm center. Erin pulled her to her even tighter and bucked in orgasm, their eyes never breaking contact.

"Addison? Addison?"

Hearing her name called snapped Addison out of her daydream.

"What? I'm sorry. What did you say?"

Stacy, a middle-aged mother of four, was looking at her

enviously. They'd chatted last night, and she was standing beside her this morning. "I don't know where you went, girl, but next time take me with you."

Addison blushed, and Stacy winked at her.

"I said CaroleAnn is here."

Instead of following Stacy, Addison made the mistake of looking at Erin. Judging by her expression, Addison knew her stroll down Erotic Memory Lane was written all over her face.

CHAPTER SIX

Erin's knees were weak as she walked to the pile of lumber stacked neatly to her right. Not only had her heart skipped a beat or two when she saw Addison this morning, it had completely stopped when she realized what had to have been going on in her mind. No one got that look on their face thinking about what's for dinner.

Holy shit, Erin thought. I almost came just watching her. As it was, her briefs were wet, and if she didn't get herself under control, it would be a long, chafing day.

Erin had been aroused more times than she could count, but never to this extent. One wrong move, and given the way her jeans were rubbing her clit, it would all be over. Maybe she could get Addison into a private area for just a minute. That's all it would take, but she knew she would want so much more. Erin looked around. Shit. Nothing but waist-high piles of lumber.

"Didn't we have this talk last night?" Susie was standing beside her.

"Did they teach you that look in mom school?" Erin asked, staring at the frown on her sister-in-law's forehead. She had never known Susie to say a harsh word until she began disciplining her children. With four kids, the older they got, the more mischief they got into, and she had perfected the expression.

"Yes, they did, and I got an A."

"No doubt."

"Don't try to sidestep me, young lady," Susie scolded her.

"Hey. I'm older than you. Shouldn't you be respecting me?" Erin enjoyed teasing her.

"I do, and that's why I'm trying to keep you out of trouble."

"This is the kind of trouble I like—a lot." Erin raised and lowered her eyebrow several times.

"Don't be a pig." Susie gave her a playful slap on the arm.

"Why do you always hit me?" Erin asked, faking pain.

"Because I can't hit anyone else."

"Why don't you take it out on a nail?"

"Because someone needs to knock some sense into you."

"I have plenty of sense, thank you very much. It's a good orgasm I'm in need of."

Susie's expression turned serious, and she looked to her left, then her right. She leaned in and whispered into Erin's ear. "I'm sorry, but I have a husband and four kids at home. I'm afraid all my time is booked."

Erin laughed. "You dummy. Let's get to work."

CaroleAnn gave a few last-minute instructions, and after verifying all the crewmembers were in attendance, she handed out the assignments.

Erin and Susie, along with four other women, would be building the exterior wall on the north side of one of the houses. The women gathered around a large pile of neatly stacked 2x4s. A tall, very attractive African American woman in jeans, work boots, and a faded Beatles T-shirt approached.

"Good morning, ladies. My name is Charlotte, and I'm your foreman on this build."

"Thank God. I was hoping one of you knew what you're doing. I'm clueless," one of the women commented. All the women laughed, nerves skittering through the group.

"Shouldn't that be forewoman?" someone behind Erin asked. Another one snickered, and several nodded in agreement.

"Technically, I suppose so, but personally I don't care. I'm more concerned with what a person can do versus what they're called." That ridiculous issue being settled, Charlotte continued.

"We don't want anyone to get hurt on this job. You're here to have fun and build a house for a wonderful lady and her kids. I don't want to make anyone uncomfortable or be embarrassed, but I need to know your experience and comfort level on doing this kind of work. We're going to be hammering, cutting, measuring, and performing a lot of physical labor."

Each woman confessed her experience, followed by Susie, then Erin.

"I've done some minor remodeling on my place but nothing quite so extensive, so I know the basics. I'm pretty handy with tools, and I take direction very well. After watching the YouTube videos, my comfort factor is about a nine."

In addition to signing all the paperwork, their pre-work consisted of watching several videos that demonstrated the basics of building a house and jobsite safety. Erin had a lot of common sense, but she was grateful that safety seemed to be the number-one priority. The last thing she needed was to get hurt and not be able to work.

"Okay. Great," Charlotte said, sliding her tape measure out of her tool belt. "Let's start with the basics. How to read a tape measure."

Charlotte spent the next few minutes giving a primer on how to accurately measure, hold, and swing a hammer.

"Why don't we use one of those things that nail automatically?" someone asked.

"It's called a nail gun," Charlotte replied. "We're not using it for a few reasons. First, they are very dangerous, and, no offense to anyone, but none of you know how to use one. Someone could get seriously hurt. Second, they're awfully expensive, and we can't afford to have one for everyone, including the air compressors to make them work. We have a few for some parts of the build, but only those with experience will handle them."

Erin didn't envy Charlotte her job. She had no interest in babysitting six woman all day, however attractive they might be.

She just wanted to exercise her muscles and get to work to make a difference.

"Break up into teams of two, and let's get this wall up," Charlotte said, clapping her hands twice for emphasis.

CHAPTER SEVEN

G od, I've missed this," Addison mumbled when her hammer connected with another nail. Framing was her favorite part of construction. It was simple but hard work and showed almost immediate results. If it weren't for her father's need to have her take over the management of the company, Addison would've made a career out of what she was doing right now. She pulled another 2x4 from the stack, took the tape measure out of her pouch, measured and marked, then remeasured. Her father had drilled this process into her the first time she picked up a saw. Measure twice and cut once was the most common phrase in the building industry and always applicable.

"You have more expertise than you let on."

Addison had been so in the zone with what she was doing, she hadn't heard her crew foreman, Michelle, approach.

"My father thought all his kids needed to know the basics, including his daughters." Addison said, not giving much away. Michelle looked at her critically.

"You know more than the basics," Michelle commented "You work three times as fast as anyone else, you hit the nail on the head every time and can sink it in three strikes. Your boots aren't new, and that belt," Michelle pointed to her tool belt, "doesn't get broken in like that sitting on a shelf in the garage."

Addison didn't respond. What was the point? It was all true, and she didn't need to hide what she knew, just who she was.

"I've enjoyed building all my life. I like keeping my skills up."

"Well, I'm glad you're on my crew, Addison. I look forward to working with you."

Addison breathed a sigh of relief. It wasn't a matter of life and death that no one find out who she was, but she just wanted to relax and do what she loved.

"Can you show me how to do that?" Addison turned and found one of the women on her crew standing beside her. She thought her name was Joy but couldn't be sure. What she was sure of was that she was a petite blonde with flawless skin and long false eyelashes. Who wore false eyelashes on a construction site?

"Do what?" Addison asked.

"How to hold a hammer. I must be doing something wrong because I can't hit the nail, and after two or three times my arm hurts." She slowly stroked her forearm to emphasize her point. Addison knew it was to attract her attention and make her imagine it was she who was stroking her tan skin.

The woman's tone was that of a woman pretending to be helpless, which was a complete turnoff.

"Sure. Let me see what you're doing." She decided to give the woman the benefit of the doubt. She'd been much too jaded lately about women and their intentions.

Addison watched her take a few swings before stopping her. "Here. Let me show you," Addison said, demonstrating the correct way. The woman leaned closer, almost too close to be safe.

"You mean like this?" she asked, leaning in, her breasts touching Addison's arm. She made a flailing attempt to hit a nail.

"No. You need to grip it like this," Addison said, demonstrating once again.

"Can you show me again?" the woman asked when Addison handed her back the hammer. She stepped even closer, holding the handle, her message clear that she wanted Addison to put her hand over the top of hers to show her the proper grip.

Addison knew what game the woman was playing, and she had no interest. She was in an awkward position but placed her hand over Joy's anyway. Joy stepped closer, their bodies touching.

Addison demonstrated a few more times, knowing damn good and well Joy was not paying attention. Addison felt the heat coming off Joy's body and was not at all tempted to lean into it. She was not interested, and even if she was, she didn't need that complication on a job site. She stepped back, letting go.

"Now all you need to do is practice." Addison turned her back and started to measure a piece of wood, hoping the woman got the hint.

"Lunch," CarolAnn called from the top of another of the many piles of lumber a few hours later. Addison slid her hammer into the holder on her belt, something she did without even thinking. She retrieved her Igloo lunchbox from the back seat of the Jeep and joined her crew in the shade. She'd just finished drinking half a bottle of water when Pam, one of the other women, spoke.

"What do you do for a living, Addison?"

Addison tensed then relaxed, seeing nothing but sincere interest in the woman's eyes. "I work in a real estate office. What about you?" she asked, immediately deflecting the attention from herself.

"You're a dichotomy, Addison." Joy interrupted before Pam had a chance to answer. Was she trying to impress Addison with her big words?

"What does that mean?" Sylvia asked. Sylvia was going to be the homeowner of the house they were building. Addison couldn't tell how old she was because of the lines of experience and a hard life etched on her face. Her fourteen-year-old son was one of the few males on the project.

"It means complete opposites," Joy said smugly. "Her clothes are worn from experience, and she holds a hammer better than all of us combined. But her lunch box is brand new, and she drives a very expensive ride."

Addison glanced at her crew, and everyone was looking at her expectantly.

"I've done these builds before, so I have the gear. I live in Arizona, so I didn't pack my lunch box, and my ride is a rental. I came here because who doesn't want to be in paradise?"

Conversation died down as they ate, and Addison realized

she missed the lunchtime camaraderie that typically came with the same people working side by side for weeks and sometimes years. However, with this group, there was no conversation about kids, sports, or trucks and no complaints about the Mrs. They were all too tired to discover if they had anything in common other than their desire to help.

Addison looked at her watch. Fifteen minutes left in their lunch break. She lay down on the soft dirt. She'd been bent over all morning, and it felt good to straighten her back and work out all the kinks. She'd be comfortably sore tonight and had a large bag of Epson salts ready to go into a hot bath. A good long soak, and a couple of Advil, and she'd be good to go.

It was quiet, the noise of hammers, saws, and excited chatter no longer existent. She closed her eyes and tried to make her mind relax, but Addison was not good at simply relaxing. She was always busy doing something, whether it was the pile of paperwork that never shrank, the endless contract reviews, or the remodel she was doing on her own house. Her brain never stopped. Even when her body was exhausted after making love, she didn't fall asleep. Maybe that was why she couldn't keep a girlfriend. She didn't have much time for dating or lying around by the pool or on the couch channel-surfing. She needed to be active and had yet to find a woman who was the same.

What's with that *yet*, Addison, she thought. Didn't Debra tell you to stop looking? Debra had been her college roommate, and even though they lived a country apart, they still talked regularly. Just last week she'd told Addison that as soon as she stopped looking, Ms. Right would knock on her front door. With her track record, Addison would open the back door to Ms. Wrong, again.

Addison must have dozed off, because she was startled when someone nudged the bottom of her boot.

"Time to get back at it, Bobbie."

Addison shaded her eyes, Joy standing at her feet.

"Bobbie?"

"Yeah. You know. The female version of Bob the Builder," Joy said, winking at her.

Addison hated being called Bob, Bobbie, or anything other than her real name, except by her grandmother, who called her Addie. The reference to the children's cartoon of Bob the Builder and his adventures on a construction site was old news. If she had a dollar for every time she'd been called that, she could probably finance three more houses on this project.

She got up, her knees cracking. "Clever," Addison said, trying to sound casual. She'd had Joy pegged before the first morning break. What she really wanted to say was, "Joy, you're a pain in the ass. Shut the fuck up and leave me alone."

❖

"So, what do you think?" Susie asked, then took a final swig of her Coke.

I think she's sexy as hell, mysterious, intriguing, and fascinating. She can swing a hammer like nobody's business and is much more experienced in this than she lets on. I want to make her sweat like that.

"Get your head out of the gutter, Erin."

"What? I didn't say anything."

"You didn't have to. It's written all over your face what you're thinking about that one." She tilted her head in the direction of Addison. "Plus, I know how your mind works and the type of woman you're interested in. How do you run a successful business with women in bikinis in your face all day? Do you ever think about anything else? Are you sex crazed? A sexaholic? Do you *ever* sleep alone?" Susie shook her head and rolled her eyes.

"Do you want an answer to any of those questions?"

"I will admit she's nothing like your normal conquests."

"Conquests? That's a little harsh, don't you think, Susie? The women I see are with me because they want to be—not because I seduced them and they had no idea what they were doing."

"I've witnessed your charms more than a few times."

"I can't help it if women fall at my feet," Erin said, joking.

"Fall into your bed is more accurate."

"Isn't that the whole point?" In her book there was nothing wrong with that view, if both parties were on the same dance card.

"There's more to sex than just sex," Susie commented.

"Do tell, Mrs. Married to My Brother for Sixteen Years."

"It's emotional. The connection is here." Susie pointed to her heart. "Not just between your legs. That's why they call it making love."

"And that's why I have sex. I'm not in love with the woman. I'm sorry, but I don't feel anything north of between my legs, as you so accurately described it. I'm sorry if you think that makes me crass or insensitive or just plain slutty, but—"

"Erin," Susie said, suddenly serious. "You know that's not at all what I think."

Erin relaxed. When did this conversation turn from teasing to uncomfortable?

"I love you like my own sister, and it's because of that I just want you to be happy."

"I am happy," Erin said, feeling like she had to defend herself.

"Look. I had just sex lots of times before I met your brother," Susie said, using her fingers to make quotes. "And we even had just sex many times after I met him. I know the difference, and there's absolutely no comparison."

"I'm not like you, Susie. I'm not interested in finding the one and living happily ever after." Erin mimicked Susie's air quotes. She had yet to meet anyone she wanted to spend any extensive amount of time with, let alone marry.

"Are you afraid you'll get bored?"

"I'm not afraid of anything." Again, Erin felt like she was justifying her actions. "But I know me, and I will get bored with the same woman."

"Not if she's the right woman."

Erin shifted from looking at Susie to immediately finding Addison. Her heart jumped.

"Why does everyone who's in love think everybody else needs to be? What makes you think there's only one person out there for someone?"

Why did she feel jealous when she saw Little Miss Thing making a play for Addison? More than a few women couldn't keep their eyes off Addison, and several had flirted with her even though it was barely noon.

"She's not your type."

"What do you mean? I don't have a type."

"We all have a type. The other women you've been with have been movie-star beautiful. High cheekbones, perfect body, could-be-a-runway-model beautiful."

"So? I like beautiful women."

"Other than the fact that she's tall, there's nothing really special about her."

"When did you become so shallow?"

"I'm not. I'm just telling you what I see."

"Well, what do they say? Beauty is in the eye of the beholder?"

"And it's always more than skin deep," Susie said before standing up. "Let's get back at it. If I sit here much longer, I won't want to get up."

Erin tossed the remains of her lunch into the trash can and took a detour toward Addison on her return to her job site. Miss Thing was talking to her, and Addison did not look happy.

"Did I come a little too close to the truth, Bobbie?"

Bobbie? I thought her name was Addison. Erin sensed tension between them. Addison looked annoyed, the woman facing her obnoxious.

"Look, Joy. I don't care what you call me or what you think I am. I'm here to help Sylvia Morales and her boys have a place to call home. Now, if you'll excuse me."

Addison turned her back on the woman and walked away.

"What a bitch," the woman hissed.

"Come on, Joy." The woman beside her grabbed Joy's arm, pulling her in the opposite direction. "Let it go."

Erin hurried to catch up to Addison.

"Hey, Addison."

Addison stopped and slowly turned around. For an instant Erin thought she looked relieved that she wasn't the obnoxious one.

"How's it going?" *How's it going? If that's the best you can do, you're definitely off your game, Erin.*

Allison's face relaxed. "It's good." She tilted her head as if to jog her memory. "Erin, right?"

Erin's heart skittered that Addison remembered her name. She felt like she was in fifth grade; *ooh, she remembers my name.*

"Right. What does CarolAnn have you working on?" Erin knew exactly what Addison had been doing all morning.

"I'm at house number two. We're constructing the west wall. How about you?"

Erin pointed over her shoulder. "North wall. Lots of windows. Lots of measuring and headers and footers."

Addison chuckled. "Headers, yes, but footers are called baseplates."

"Right, baseplate, got it. I guess that's why we have a foreman watching over us pretty closely."

"Even though we're volunteers, the house still has to be structurally sound and pass inspection."

Erin was a good bullshitter and could talk to anyone about anything, but she couldn't think of anything else to say.

"Well, be careful," Addison said, turning to leave. "If you're not used to this kind of work, accidents happen when you start getting tired."

"Yeah. Thanks. You too." *Jesus, Erin, you have gone and lost your mind?*

The rest of the afternoon flew by, and Erin was surprised when CarolAnn passed the word that it was quitting time.

"Enough for today, ladies. Look at what you've accomplished." CarolAnn spread her arms as if taking it all in. She continued, but Erin wasn't paying attention. She was looking for an opening.

Erin had chided herself all afternoon for being a tongue-tied teenager. She felt no better than the blonde and her transparent seduction. She was much more experienced and smoother and more sincere in her interactions. She didn't have a well-rehearsed opening line, or any line for that matter. She didn't lie or fudge the truth when she complimented a woman. She didn't pretend to be interested in her hobbies or political views. She didn't need to scam a woman to get what she wanted. Then why did she stumble all over herself like a newborn animal caught trying to get her feet under her? The crowd of women started breaking up, and Addison drifted away. Erin made her move.

"Quite a day, wasn't it?" Erin said, quickly catching up to Addison.

Addison removed her hat and sunglasses and wiped her face with a damp cloth. The most crystal-clear blue eyes Erin had ever seen looked at her and her heart skittered.

"Yes, it was. We all got a lot done." Addison stopped and looked behind her. At least the two external walls that were up, held in place with 2x4s angled and secured into the cement floor. The house Addison has been working on had all four walls up.

"Your house is way ahead of the rest of us," Erin commented. "All four walls are standing."

"I guess everything just fell into place a little bit better," Addison said modestly. Other women would have bragged about their superiority on the job.

"I saw you helping a few people." The buxom blonde leaning into Addison flashed in Erin's mind, causing her to see green around the edges of her brain.

"We're all here to learn and have a good time."

"It's obvious you've got more to teach them than to learn," Erin said. "You swing that hammer like a pro." Erin was trying to compliment Addison, but judging by her expression it appeared her praise was making her uncomfortable.

"Thanks, but it's all just about practice more than anything else." Sometime during the brief conversation, they'd started walking again and were almost to Addison's Jeep.

"Did I see you at Lahaina Pizza Company the other night? You were sitting at the bar."

Addison looked surprised, then recovered. "Yes. I think so."

"It's a great place, isn't it?"

"Yes. It's one of my favorite places when I come to town."

"Do you come here often?"

Addison's eyebrows rose. "You did not just ask me that?"

The absurdity of what she just said hit Erin. She flushed in embarrassment.

"No. I meant, do you come to the island often?" That was only slightly better.

"I've been here maybe half a dozen times. It's one of my favorite places to rest and relax."

"Would you like to get a beer or maybe dinner? We can celebrate our first day, and you can tell me your other favorite places to go."

Erin was more nervous than she could remember. She'd asked out dozens, maybe hundreds of women in the past twenty-five years and couldn't remember another time she'd wanted a yes so much. Even after she discovered the magic of orgasm, she hadn't wanted a woman to say yes as badly as she wanted it now. What was up with that?

"Thanks, but I have plans."

Erin masked her disappointment. She'd thought they were clicking, and the way they'd connected at LPC, she was sure the evening would continue. If she played her cards right, she was hoping it wouldn't end until the morning.

"That's twice you've turned me down. A girl could get a complex."

Addison studied her, and Erin's pulse raced when Addison smiled.

"I'm sure you'll get over it. Good night."

CHAPTER EIGHT

Addison breathed a sigh of relief when she pulled out of the parking lot. If she had to dodge one more thinly veiled come-on, she'd pull her hair out. Except for one from Erin. She was definitely out of practice evading unwanted advances on a job site. Whether from men or women, they were all the same—distracting, and a royal pain in the ass, to say nothing of against the law. Addison had never had to play that card on the job. She always managed to make her point perfectly clear. She also knew that, unfortunately and equally illegal, was that the resulting working conditions could be intolerable. Bradbury Construction had won several diversity and equality awards for setting the standards for equal employment and a workplace free from harassment and intimidation. She dealt with any complaints quickly, firing both men and women when anything offensive occurred.

She looked to her left to make sure traffic was clear and noticed Joy and her girl posse looking at her. They were five in total, and each one had made a play for her at least once throughout the day. Joy had the advantage, as she was on Addison's crew, while the others had been AWOL from theirs. Addison wasn't self-centered, and she certainly wasn't a clairvoyant, but she did have a pretty good sixth sense that they had a wager on who would score first, and she was the prize. At least Erin didn't resort to subterfuge and what Addison had thought of as feminine wiles to get what she wanted. Erin's intentions were clear. She didn't play the helpless female or lean into her when asking for help or pretend that she didn't know how to hold a hammer or measure or mark a board.

Addison might be rusty catching an invitation tossed her way, but she clearly knew one when she saw it. And she saw it every time Erin looked at her. Most disturbing was that she felt it as well. Long-dormant butterflies in her stomach came to life, and her strong legs felt a little weak, her concentration scattered, and her focus blurred. She was a walking job-site safety hazard. Between dodging unwanted advances and reacting to Erin, Addison was surprised she still had all ten fingers. As it was, her thumb was already turning a dark shade of purple, a color she hadn't self-inflicted in years.

Addison had almost given in to Erin's invitation to have a beer, to just unwind at the end of a long day. Many nights after work she'd help empty several pitchers of beer, laugh, and catch a few minutes of whatever game was on the TV in the bar with her crew. Now she spent the end of most days at her desk at home finishing must-do's and preparing for the next day.

When had her life become nothing but work? Did her relationships fail because she was always working, or did she use work to fill her time so she didn't have to try again? Addison could barely remember her last vacation a few years ago. She'd rented an RV and spent two weeks in Yosemite, staying literally off the grid except for every morning when she logged in and responded to anything marked urgent. She discovered a love for fishing, catch and release, of course; filled her lungs with crisp, clean mountain air; and watched the clouds drift across the blue sky from her hammock. She fell asleep counting the stars every night.

Back at her room, she showered and carried a glass, a bottle of wine, and a chair onto the almost-deserted beach. A photographer was taking advantage of the waning sunset photographing a family, their kids splashing in the water. Would she ever have photos like that on a desk or walls at home? Would she ever experience the joy of Disneyland through the eyes of a child or cheer with bursting pride from the sidelines? Not if she kept up the way she was living now. Did she want to? If she did and she didn't change something, she would do it all alone.

Maybe she'd take a couple of kids out of the foster system and give them a good home. She toyed with the idea of adopting a baby from a foreign country, but that was too frightening to seriously contemplate. With her job, how could she raise a child? Good grief, she thought. Women do it every day. You figure it out. That would definitely put an even more serious crimp in her dating life. What dating life? She had none. Last year, her administrative assistant had brought her daughter to the office until she needed more attention. Her crib was beside her desk, and the first time she breast-fed the baby during a staff meeting was shocking. "Get over it, everybody," she said to the stunned executives around the table. "It's a food source."

Addison left the chair outside the patio door, brushed off her feet, and went inside. She opened the windows to let the cool night air circulate, and after brushing her teeth, she crawled between the covers, hoping she wouldn't dream of a dark-haired woman with enticing eyes.

CHAPTER NINE

"You look like hell," Susie commented as Erin was buckling up. Erin was used to waking at four thirty, but when her alarm went off this morning, she'd hit the snooze button three times. She'd had to rush around and pack her lunch, and Susie had to honk twice before she was out the door. She'd left her car at the dealership last night for some recall work, and she and Susie were carpooling for a few days. It was the second day, and she was exhausted.

"If you ever wanted to be a lesbian, leading with that line will get you nowhere."

"I'm perfectly happy in my heterosexual world, thank you very much, but you still look like hell. Don't tell me you had enough energy last night to go out and get some? I was barely able to take a shower before I crashed."

"Not that my sex life is any of your business, but no. I just didn't sleep well." Erin didn't add that it was because she'd dreamed of a gorgeous woman with a tool belt. "I thought I was in pretty good shape, but I'm sore in places I didn't know I had."

"I know," Susie said. "I groaned like an old lady when I got out of bed. Today is going to be a long day."

They broke early, the storm clouds that had been overhead threatening to burst open any moment. Erin had kept an eye out for Addison and had only seen her twice, once when the same blonde had come sniffing around again. Addison must have brushed her off because she stomped away, her anger obvious for everyone to see.

Erin wanted to try her luck with Addison again. Maybe they could spend the late afternoon over a fruity drink at one of her favorite watering holes. She left disappointed, Susie ready to go before she had a chance to talk to her.

The next morning Erin was up early, having tossed and turned most of the night. Each time she closed her eyes, a new image of Addison flashed in front of her. There was the time she reached up to steady a piece of wood and her shirt pulled out of her pants, showing her stomach. The way she smiled and patiently showed someone how to cut a piece of wood. The way the sun caught on the highlights in her hair, and how she proudly surveyed her work. Each sighting was more interesting than the last. Other than her interactions with her crew, Addison had kept to herself most of the day. From what Erin could see, she was a good teacher, showing the women the proper way to do things when they asked for her help. She patiently demonstrated whatever was necessary, then went back to what she'd been working on.

Erin hadn't quite finished her coffee when they pulled into the dirt lot they were using as a parking lot. She hustled to grab her lunch and gear.

"See you in a few," she said to Susie as she hurried out of the van.

"Good morning," she said as Addison got out of her Jeep.

"Good morning. Ready for another day?"

"Absolutely," Erin said honestly. She fell into step beside Addison as they crossed the street.

"Sore?"

"A little," Erin lied. She'd had a hard time getting out of bed this morning. "Just in the muscles I don't normally use."

"It's pretty physical work."

"You mean when I'm not hitting my thumb?" Erin held up her thumb that was sporting a wonderful shade of purple as evidence.

"Ouch. That'll hurt if you hit it again today."

"It hurts now, and I don't intend to hit it, but then again, I hadn't planned on it yesterday either. Now, admittedly, I'm a little gun-shy," Erin said.

"Use a pair of pliers."

"I'm sorry. I'm not following. A pair of pliers?"

"To hold the nail. That way you'll save your thumb until your hand-eye coordination improves."

They arrived at the main assembly area as they did yesterday, and CarolAnn was calling them together.

Addison reached into her tool belt that she'd slung over her shoulder and handed Erin a pair of needle-nose pliers.

"Here. You can use these."

"Thanks, but what if you need them?"

"Then I guess I'll just have to come find you."

Erin's stomach flip-flopped at the gleam of interest in Addison's eyes. It looked like her game might be doing just fine.

A few days later, when CarolAnn called lunch, Erin knew she should eat, but all she wanted to do was take a nap. She must have dozed off because she was startled when a voice above her spoke.

"You really should eat something."

Addison was silhouetted in the sun, her features shadowed. Other than the few words they'd exchanged on the first day or two, they hadn't really talked. Erin had made a point of being near Addison several times over the past few days and doing what she thought of as mild flirting—nothing too serious if Addison wasn't interested. Just a quick comment as she walked by. She wanted Addison, and it looked like her play might be working.

"You need to fuel your body," Addison said.

Erin shadowed her eyes when Addison sat down beside her. "My body is making a scheduled pit stop at the moment."

"Eat first, then rest."

Addison opened Erin's lunch box and handed her the sandwich she had thrown together that morning. "Eat."

After she struck out the other day, the last thing she expected was Addison sitting beside her and practically feeding her. She might be exhausted but knew enough to take advantage of this golden opportunity.

"Do you always take care of strangers like this?" Erin asked, opening her sandwich bag.

"You're not really a stranger," Addison answered. "We work together."

Erin heated as Addison's gaze ran over her.

"That, and you look like you really need it."

"Gee. You really know how to make a girl feel pretty."

"Well, you are," Addison replied, shifting her eyes to something across the street.

"Needy or pretty?"

Addison turned and looked at her, her eyes serious. "No to the former. I think you can probably take care of yourself. And yes to the latter."

"If no to the needy part, why are you sitting beside me and telling me to eat?"

"Because who doesn't want to have lunch with a pretty girl?"

"I wasn't fishing for a compliment, but thank you."

Addison leaned back against a pile of lumber. "Do I need to worry that that cheerleader I saw you getting out of the car with is going to swing her hammer at me?"

"What? Who? Susie?" Erin reflected on the scene this morning. When Susie had parked her car, they'd been joking around, and Erin gave Susie a quick kiss on the lips, and said, "Have a good day at the office, honey."

"No, no. Susie is my sister-in-law. My brother would skin me if I ever made a move on his wife, which I absolutely wouldn't. I'm not even the slightest bit interested in straight women, and definitely not her." Erin knew she was rambling, but Addison's concern intrigued her. "My car is in the shop, so we're carpooling for a few days."

Addison kept looking at her, her gaze penetrating.

"I don't poach," she said seriously, heat in her eyes.

"I appreciate that, but there is no one. You?"

"I find it hard to believe a woman as pretty as you is unattached."

"Are you calling me a liar?" Erin smiled, showing Addison she wasn't as serious as her words.

"No, it's just that…"

"Take my advice, Ms. Sexy Swinging a Hammer. Take advantage of what's right in front of you before it's gone."

"And would I regret it if I didn't?" Addison's eyes sparkled.

Erin's heart skipped, and her head spun. When had things changed? Every other time Addison had been giving her the brush-off, but today she was hitting on her.

"That's for you to decide. I know I would if I were you. But you haven't answered my question."

"In that case you definitely need to eat your lunch. Gotta keep your strength up so I can buy you that beer at quitting time."

Addison hadn't intended to approach Erin, but somehow, she'd ended up here. She'd known what Erin was up to when she crossed her path, and she'd done her best to ignore her moves. However, as much as she tried, she was drawn to her, and she had spent most of the past forty-eight hours trying to figure out why. Addison was tired of fighting her attraction to Erin. What was wrong with a little vacation fling? She was single and had no responsibilities or obligations that would be hurt by experiencing Erin's touch, inhaling her scent, tasting her lips, her skin, her wetness.

Finally, she gave in and just decided to go for it. It would just be a fling, if it even got that far. She was only here for a few weeks. She doubted Erin lived in Phoenix and came here for the same reason. They'd never see each other again.

Addison stretched out her legs, leaned her head back, and closed her eyes. She felt Erin's eyes on her and wondered what conclusion she was drawing. Did she think her feet looked huge in her work boots, her belly a little too big? Her hips a bit too wide? Did she see the gray hairs at her temple and the lines around her eyes? Did she look as old as she sometimes felt? Thirty-seven wasn't old, but she didn't turn heads like she did in her twenties, or even a few years ago.

Addison was proud of the woman she'd become over the last fifteen years. Her taste for cheap beer, babes, and staying out all night had slowly matured into good beer, better wine, women who had their shit together, and, unless occupied by said woman, being asleep by eleven. She finally understood herself and no longer settled for anything other than exactly what she wanted. So where did Erin fit in? She looked at least ten years younger and had a rock-hard body and eyes that sparkled with interest in everything around her. What did she do for a living? She had a fabulous tan, but who didn't, living on Maui?

Addison had seen a few women try to get Erin's attention, and who wouldn't? Erin looked like the outdoorsy type, if you were into that sort of thing, and Addison definitely was. She'd dated professional women, the ones who wore expensive suits and overpriced designer shoes, but they hadn't held her attention for long. Actually no one had held her attention except Erin, and she had barely spoken to her. At least once a day Addison hit her thumb with her hammer either looking for Erin or looking at her. Her attraction to her was extraordinarily different than it had been for anyone else. A whistle blew.

"Back to work," Addison said, rising and extending her hand to Erin.

"Do I have to?"

"The sooner we start, the sooner we finish and can have that cold beer."

Erin grabbed Addison's hand and jumped up, stopping inches from her. With a slight movement, Addison could be kissing the lips that had taunted her for days. If she leaned forward just a little, she would feel Erin's breasts pressed against hers. She inhaled her scent, apricot and good, clean woman sweat. Her head spun, and before she had a chance to grab Erin like she would a life raft, Erin stepped away laughing.

"Well, when you put it that way."

CHAPTER TEN

They found an empty high-top table in a corner of a quiet bar Erin had directed her to.

"Have you lived in Maui your entire life?" Addison asked.

"No. I was born in Japan. My dad was in the Navy, and we lived all over the world. My parents settled in Honolulu after he retired, and I came here about fifteen years ago."

"Where was the most interesting place you ever lived?" Addison found it fascinating that they were having a typical get-to-know-you conversation when this wasn't going to be a long-term thing, nor did it have any long-term potential whatsoever. But she was interested in Erin as a person. Did she cry at sad movies? What was her favorite music? Did she like to read, dance, play poker? She wanted her views on everything from butter versus margarine to global warming. She wanted to know everything about her. She couldn't recall ever being this curious about a woman.

The blatant chemistry between them was undeniable. The sexual tension was palatable, and they should be discovering what made each of them moan in pleasure and squirm with need, not their favorite color and vegetable.

Addison watched Erin as she talked. Her eyes twinkled when she was amused and darkened when she was curious or smoldered with desire. And when Erin looked at her, Addison felt like she was the only woman in the world, enjoying the feeling that she had Erin's complete focus and attention. Those thoughts frightened her, and the way she felt when she was with Erin scared the holy hell out of her. It made no sense. There was no future here. So why did she want more?

"What do you do when you're not building houses?" she asked, just to hear Erin's voice again.

"I own a snorkeling boat."

"Like take-tourists-out snorkeling boat?"

"Uh-huh," Erin answered, biting into a fried mozzarella stick. Watching her mouth mesmerized Addison.

"What's its name?" Addison asked, trying to get her head back into some sort of normalcy. "Maybe I've been out on it before. I try to go snorkeling every time I come to the island. However," Addison let her eyes wander over Erin, "if you were the captain, I would've remembered." Addison's blood warmed. She liked telling Erin how she felt about her. Erin's eyes burned; her compliment had hit its mark.

Erin considered Addison's question for a moment. She had a minute of panic that she didn't remember if she'd ever been with her. She'd forgotten more women than she could remember. A pang of guilt pierced her.

No way could she have forgotten Addison. First, her name would've stood out. Second, she was a woman who knew what she wanted, how to get it, and, most important, probably what to do with it when she did.

She was drawn to Addison in a way she'd never been before with any other woman. Maybe it was her sophistication. She was by far in a very different league than any woman she'd ever met. Addison carried herself like a very confident and successful woman. Erin could picture her all dressed up with expensive shoes and a name-brand briefcase, commanding a boardroom. And that was just plain sexy. And, my God, the way she looked in her jeans and boots was nothing short of mouthwatering.

"*Westwind.* Actually, I have two boats, but I do take a day off now and then." Erin had agonized for months over buying a second boat. It would increase her income but also her expenses and responsibilities and worries. Leilani had wanted to go in on it with her, but Erin didn't want the commitment of a partner, no matter how trustworthy she was.

"I didn't think you had an office job."

"How could you tell?"

"The tan line on your legs. You don't get that sitting behind a desk all day."

Erin's heart skipped. Addison had been looking at her legs at the briefing the other night.

"You'd laugh if you saw me naked."

Addison's eyes smoldered, and Erin realized what she'd just said. It wasn't a practiced line or one designed to tease. It just came out because she felt so comfortable with Addison.

"I don't think I'd be laughing if you were naked."

The earth spun, and Erin had to grab on to the edge of the table to keep from toppling over. The look in Addison's eyes, the intensity and directness of her words were the most erotically powerful thing she had ever heard. She had been the pursuer, and now the roles had reversed.

Erin wanted to crawl up inside Addison and never come out. She wanted to breathe her air and be in her skin, and those thoughts were terrifying. She had to run, very far and very, very fast, but she couldn't move, didn't want to move. Erin told herself to breathe. In, out, repeat. In, out, repeat until the light-headedness that had threatened to allow her to do something stupid and completely out of character passed.

"No," Addison said, breaking the trance. "No, I don't think I've ever sailed with you. I would have remembered."

Erin started to breathe again, but it was far from normal. She was relieved she'd dodged both bullets Addison had tossed her way but knew she wasn't immune to her. God. Just being in the same room with her was enough to throw her over the edge. The welcome session and the few moments at the restaurant proved that. She decided to use humor to break the wave of feeling that threatened to pull her under.

"Well, I won't hold that against you."

"What would you hold against me?"

"Anything you like."

The seriousness in Addison's tone and the blaze in her eyes gave no doubt what "anything" meant. Erin laughed, but her stomach had jumped to somewhere in the middle of her throat. Heat coursed through her, and she realized Addison was waiting for an answer.

"If that's a line, I'd say no." Again, something she'd never worried about when she wanted a woman. She didn't mind getting lines from a woman if it would ultimately get her where she wanted to be—between the sheets.

"I don't do lines."

"And you don't poach either." Erin's voice didn't sound like her own, her throat pinched with emotion.

Addison shook her head, her eyes never leaving Erin's.

"You're a very honorable woman, Addison."

"You say that like it's a novelty."

Erin thought for a moment. She had a few close friends and family that she trusted with her life. The women she slept with obviously didn't fall anywhere near that category. But why should they? It took Erin's breath away to think about what her life would be like if Addison were in it. Every day would be exciting and a challenge that would never grow old.

Behind her carefree attitude and actions, Erin realized, her life had grown stale. It was the same thing every day. She got up far too early, got the boat ready, played tour guide, and went to the same places every day with a boatload of sometimes rude, stupid passengers. And that didn't even count the number of times she needed to clean up vomit. It had stopped surprising her just how many beers someone could drink before noon. Then, when her passengers disembarked, she'd clean up, stow the gear, secure the boat, and get ready for the next day. She'd go home, toss the ball to Buoy, grab something to eat, maybe find a hookup, go to bed, and start all over again the next day. An overwhelming feeling came over her that maybe she should make a change.

"Then I should be addressing you as captain," Addison said, changing the subject before Erin had a chance to answer. "Who captains your other boat?"

Erin let out a breath, relieved to be back on solid, familiar ground. The last few minutes she'd had no idea where she was.

"We can't work every day, so I have five people who are licensed."

"And how many on your crew?"

More normality, thank God. "It depends on how many paying customers I have that day. I have a minimum of four and, if it's a full house, another six."

"Wow. That's a serious outfit," Addison said, obviously impressed. "I'll bet your customers think you have the perfect job. On a boat every day getting a tan, seeing beautiful sights."

Addison looked at Erin for so long and so seriously that Erin started to get nervous again.

"But that's not the case, is it?"

Erin didn't know if she should answer Addison's astute question honestly. She decided what the hell. "No. Sometimes it's just a pain in the ass."

"Well, it is a job. And work is a four-letter word," Addison said ruefully, then winked at her.

Warmth and desire pulsed through her. Was that how Addison had felt when Erin winked at her? Erin was done thinking. She wanted to feel. The high stools allowed her to lean closer. Addison smelled like sweat and woman.

"So are sexy, kiss, moan, and sigh." Addison's eyes darkened, and the pulse in her neck beat faster with every word. "And body, legs, hand, arms, neck, eyes, and lips." Erin ran her fingertips over each body part as she named it. She cupped the back of Addison's neck, her soft hair tickling her fingers.

"True. But there's one you missed," Addison said, leaning closer.

"Do tell."

"Fuck me," Addison whispered.

Addison's breath was warm on her lips.

"I like the way you count," Erin said and closed the distance between them.

Electricity shot through Erin the instant their lips met. The kiss was tentative and soft, Addison exploring with much more patience than she had. She pulled Addison closer, and the kiss kicked up a few degrees, or ten. Sensations bombarded Erin as it continued. Tingles, burning, and butterflies all combined into one overwhelming sensation that she did not want to end.

Addison pulled away first, and Erin gasped for breath. She was light-headed and held on to Addison's arms to steady herself.

It was several moments before either one of them could speak.

"Would you like another beer?" Erin asked, not sure why. She didn't want to stay here and try to make coherent conversation. She wanted to be horizontal with Addison, now.

"No." Addison's voice was husky, her eyes smoldering.

"Something else to eat?"

Addison shook her head.

"I'm trying to be a good host. You're on my island, after all."

"I've already told you what I want." Addison's voice was exactly the same tone as when she said "fuck me."

Erin tossed a fifty-dollar bill onto the bar with one hand and took Addison's with the other.

Chapter Eleven

The ride from the bar to Erin's place was quiet; the only words spoken were Erin's directions. Desire drummed through Addison because she knew what was going to happen as soon as they got there.

They got out of the Jeep and didn't touch as they walked toward the front door. It thrilled Addison to see Erin's hands fumble with her keys. It always amazed her that she could make someone crazy with desire. In her more reflective moments, she wondered if her partner was excited about being with *her* or if she was just naturally reacting to stimuli.

The need to kiss Erin was overwhelming, and she reached for her. Very quickly they were in a serious make-out session on her front porch. Erin could kiss like nobody's business, and Addison wanted to know if she did everything equally well.

Dragging her lips away from Erin's hot, demanding ones to catch her breath, she rested her forehead on Erin's. She struggled to catch her breath.

"And I thought you were an expert on swinging a hammer," Erin said, her breath a light breeze on Addison's cheek. "You're pretty good at that too. Your kiss blew out all my brain circuits."

"You're not too bad yourself." Addison chuckled. "That was a serious understatement. You practically kissed my socks off."

"If I kissed you again, would more of your clothes fall off?"

Addison stared at Erin for any sign of hesitation. What she saw instead was what was mirrored in her own eyes. Desire, heat, and more than a little determination.

"I'm sure it'll be a great start."

Addison grabbed Erin's hand when she reached for her again, and Erin shot her a confused, surprised look.

"You know I'm leaving in a few weeks?" Addison said cautiously. She didn't think Erin was the U-Haul type, and surely she knew this was not going to turn into happily-ever-after. But for some reason she needed to say it. Maybe it was *she* who needed the reminder. The way she felt when she was with Erin, the way her stomach tingled when she laughed, and other parts warmed when she looked at her was more than a little scary.

"And your point is?"

A stab of disappointment poked at Addison at the ease with which Erin asked her question. No hesitation, no second thoughts. Addison shook it off and pushed it aside and leaned into Erin again.

"My point is that we'd better get started. We don't have much time."

An excited springer spaniel greeted them with a bark and by dancing around their feet.

"Buoy, sit."

The dog obediently sat, her butt continuing to wiggle, her tail sweeping the floor. She looked up at Erin expectantly.

"Buoy, say hello."

The dog quietly barked once and spun around in a circle, then sat back down. "Buoy, shake."

The dog lifted its paw and waited, its focus on Erin for the next command.

"This is Buoy. She's nothing but pure joy and happiness."

Addison knelt and took the offered paw.

"Nice to meet you, Buoy. You are a pretty thing, just like your mama." Her fur was soft, her eyes bright with excitement.

"Okay. That's enough," Erin said, rubbing the dog on the top of her head. "Out."

The dog immediately got up and scampered from the room.

Erin grasped Addison's hand, helped her up, pulled her into her arms, and kissed her. Her pulse was hammering in all the key parts of her body. She broke away before they fucked right here in the middle of the living room.

"Now about that clock ticking…"

❖

"I need to take a shower before we do anything," Addison said as Erin led her into the bedroom.

"Not for me you don't."

"But I smell like sweat, and I have sawdust all over me. I'll get your sheets all dirty," Addison said halfheartedly.

"Trust me, Addison. The sheets are going to get dirty from more than just a little bit of your work sweat."

Addison stopped protesting when Erin yanked her shirt out of her pants and pulled it over her head. Clothes fell to the floor, and Erin backed up until her legs hit the bed. Still kissing her, Erin reached behind her and pulled down the sheet and lay down, pulling Addison with her.

She wants me in her bed. My God, she wants me *in her bed.* Addison tamped down her nerves as her excitement grew. Erin's hands were like fire on her back, roaming and never settling in one place. She moved under her with sensuous ease, and Addison tore her mouth away to lick her neck. Her skin was hot under her tongue, tasting like salt and sweat and promise. She trailed kisses down and across her chest, stopping to pay particular attention to one breast, then the other.

Erin arched into her mouth and pulled her closer. Addison's hands slid over curves and muscles, and she found Erin's particularly sensitive spots. Her ass was tight, her long legs smooth as her hands mapped out a route up and down Erin's body. Her mouth retraced the journey her hands had taken, paying attention to Erin's cues.

But it was her words that drove Addison crazy. The sound of Erin's voice, hoarse from pleasure and desire, urging her on, commanding her to "go inside, faster, harder, lick me, suck me" almost drove Addison over the edge. Addison was compelled by an unfamiliar force that made her take Erin to a level of pleasure she had never known. Time after time, Addison took her to the brink, then backed off.

Addison teased Erin, and as she reacted, she whispered in her ear, her fingers playing with her clit. "I told you I would not be laughing if I saw you naked."

Erin grabbed her hand and drove her fingers inside. "Now, Addison, now."

❖

"God, you are really good at that." Erin sighed. She lay on her side next to Addison, her head on her chest, her leg thrown over Addison's thighs. A light sheet covered them.

Addison's chuckle rumbled through her. "Thanks, but you can call me Addison."

Erin leaned up on her elbow and looked at Addison. Her eyes were closed, and a light sheen of sweat glistened on her forehead.

"You know..." Erin hesitated, then continued, "I don't even know your last name." Erin felt Addison tense. A moment of discomfort passed through her.

"Does it matter?"

Was she hiding something? Before Erin had a chance to ask, Addison spoke.

"Bradbury."

"Addison Bradbury." Erin liked saying her name. "That has a nice ring to it. Very professional sounding. You never told me what you do for a living."

"I work in real estate."

"Doing what in real estate?"

"I build houses."

"Wait." Erin sat up. The sheet fell away, the cool air drifting over her skin. Addison's eyes sparkled when they dropped to her bare breasts. Erin grew warm again.

"Bradbury as in Bradbury Construction? The firm financing the houses we're building? That Bradbury?"

"Does it matter?" Addison asked again.

"Of course it does." Addison's expression changed, and she started to get up, but Erin didn't let her. "What you're doing is fantastic. These families need decent housing, and they wouldn't get it if not for you." Erin leaned over and kissed her soundly on the mouth. "Wait until I tell Susie. She's been working with Habitat for years. She'll be thrilled."

"What are you going to tell her?" Addison's voice was serious.

"That you're responsible for this build." Erin was so excited that if Addison wasn't naked and in her bed, she'd be on the phone right now to Susie.

"I'd rather you didn't."

This time when Addison tried to get out of bed. Erin didn't stop her. She sat on the side of the bed, not moving any farther.

"Why not?" Erin asked, suddenly nervous about the change in Addison's demeanor. "Is there something you don't want people to know?"

Addison quickly turned around. "No. Of course not. My company has one of the best reputations in the business."

"Your company? Is it yours?"

"Yes."

"What you're doing is something to be proud of, Addison, not hide from."

"I'm not hiding from anything."

"Then what is it?" When she didn't answer, Erin put her hand on her back. The skin was warm and soft. "Addison?"

"I just want to relax and build a simple little house like everybody else. I don't want any fuss or special treatment."

"But everyone should be thanking you. Especially the home-owners."

"I don't want thanks. I'm doing this because I want to. These ladies need something I can give them. It's my opportunity to give back and do something I love at the same time. I'm sorry if you don't understand my position or think it's silly."

"Hey," Erin said, grabbing Addison's hand as she stood. She scampered over the messy bedding and wrapped her arms around

Addison, pressing against her. Addison was warm, the shape and texture of her now familiar.

"I think it's sweet, and your secret is safe with me."

"Erin," Addison said hesitantly.

Erin slid around and stood in front of Addison with enough distance between them that she could still think. She glanced down and marveled at Addison and the pleasure she gave her. So much for thinking clearly.

"I'm serious, Addison. I respect your position, and I won't say anything to anyone."

Addison studied her, her piercing eyes almost looking through her. She had to be tough to be a successful woman in a traditional man's industry. If anything, Erin was more fascinated with her than ever before.

Finally, Addison's expression relaxed, and she nodded. It was a huge leap of faith that Erin swore Addison would never regret. This wasn't some state secret and didn't have lives depending on it, but if it was important to Addison, it was important to her.

"Now," Erin said, stepping closer, so they touched. She felt Addison inhale at the contact. "About that shower you were so adamant about taking."

❖

"I have to go." Addison said halfheartedly. It was almost three a.m. If she didn't leave, she wouldn't get any sleep whatsoever. Not a good situation to be in on a building site.

Erin nestled into her, and Addison thought about changing her mind. She'd changed it three times already. What was one more?

"I know you do, but that means you have to get out of my bed, get dressed, and leave. None of which I am even remotely interested in you doing."

Addison rolled over on top of Erin, bracing her weight on her forearms. Erin was sleepy and had that just fabulously fucked glow about her. Addison was thrilled she was the one to put it there. Their bodies fit perfectly together.

"Neither am I, but if I don't, both of us will be a walking safety hazard in the morning."

"I know, and you are a much stronger person than I am." She kissed Addison. "Am I evil when I say I'm glad it's you who has to go and not me?"

Addison chuckled and kissed her again. Not too long or she wouldn't be able to leave, but just long enough to make a point.

"Yes. You are an evil woman. And did I ever tell you how much I like walking on the wild side?"

Erin slid her hands down her back and cupped her ass.

"Just once more," Erin said, shifting so she was straddling Addison's thigh, her arousal obvious. "Quickly."

"Who am I to refuse the request of a beautiful woman?"

Fifteen minutes later, Addison finally was in her clothes and out the front door.

Several hours later, Erin woke, and the other side of her bed was empty. She rolled over to where Addison had lain and inhaled deeply. Her scent was on the pillows, in the mussed sheets. Erin had never woken up with anyone, nor had she ever wanted to until now. She wasn't lying when she told Addison she didn't want her to leave. She, herself, had lied on many occasions when she told other women that she didn't want to leave and then promptly did. Did Addison feel that way?

Erin stretched, and erotic images of her and Addison in this big bed flashed through her mind. Addison had explored every curve of her. She'd used her fingers and tongue to arouse, to tease, to make her come. Addison clearly had an insatiable appetite, and Erin was more than willing to give her whatever she needed. Erin was not a selfish lover; at least she thought she wasn't. Admittedly, it was just as important for her to get off as it was for the woman she was with. Otherwise, what was the point?

Somewhere from the first kiss from Addison to the last lingering one, the point had changed. Make no mistake, she liked a good orgasm as much as the next woman, but pleasing Addison had been higher on her list. Much higher.

She couldn't keep her hands off her, and not because it felt good to touch her. Well, there was that, but she wanted to give Addison the almost unbearable pleasure she deserved. She wanted to be the one that made her moan with pleasure, arch her back and buck with orgasm. Erin wanted to be the name she called out when she crossed the peak and the one to hold her as she drifted down.

"Holy Christ," Erin murmured, her heart beating fast, her breath shallow. She was both aroused and frightened by her thoughts and how they made her feel. Before she had a chance to think about the situation any further, she threw back the covers and headed toward the shower—that same shower where Addison had kneeled in front of her and used her mouth and fingers to make her come. The same shower where she had pressed Addison's breasts to the cold tile and entered her from behind with one hand and rubbed her clit with the other. That same shower where…

"Good God, Erin. Get a grip." Her hands shook when she reached for the soap. The same soap that…

CHAPTER TWELVE

Addison arrived early, hoping to have a moment alone with Erin before the day began. She chuckled and shook her head. What was she going to do? Drag her behind the Jeep and put her hand in her pants? As responsive and adventurous as Erin had been last night, Addison didn't know who would be dragging who or who would come first. *"Jesus, Addison, stop."* Her briefs were already damp from thinking about Erin.

Erin was still riding with Susie, and when she got out of the van, she looked around the parking lot. Addison's heart skipped, thinking Erin was looking for her as well. She grabbed her gear and hurried out of the Jeep, making a diagonal pass and intending to meet up with them on the sidewalk. Warmth and excitement spread through her when Erin broke into a smile when she saw her. She said something to Susie, turned, and headed her way.

God, she's beautiful, Addison thought. She's funny, smart, has a quick wit and a wicked sense of humor. And she has a body that she knows exactly what to do with. Addison couldn't remember the last time, if ever, she'd looked forward to a morning after as much as she did this one. Sure, the sex had been off the charts, but she also just enjoyed being with Erin. They talked as much as their bodies communicated, which was rare for her. Sure, she would talk to women she dated, but never in bed. That was strictly for sex. Talking was much too intimate. A moment of panic seized Addison when she realized that implication.

"Good morning." Erin's voice was warm and smooth. Her eyes flared, and Addison knew what she was thinking—the same thing she'd been reliving while waiting for Erin to arrive.

"Good morning." Addison realized she wanted to say that to Erin many, many more times. Before she had a chance to think about that idea, Erin leaned in and kissed her on the cheek.

"I'd give you a proper good-morning kiss if forty women weren't watching."

"I don't mind if you don't," Addison said honestly.

Desire flared in Erin's eyes. "I'll save that for later. What I have in mind would get us arrested."

Addison groaned. "That is so not fair. I'm already wet just thinking about you, and now you've gone and done that. If I were a man, I'd have to walk around all day with a toolbox in front of me."

"I do have a toolbox at home, if you're interested?"

Addison's mouth dropped open, and her throat closed. *Holy shit.* It was going to be a long day.

Erin sat down beside Addison for lunch. The morning had dragged by, her thoughts constantly turning to what she would do with Addison when they were finally alone. Addison had chosen a spot away from the others and was partially hidden behind a pile of sheet rock. On second thought…

Erin shifted closer, scanning the area. No one was paying them any attention. She started to unbutton Addison's pants, but Addison grabbed her wrist.

"Hey."

"Shh," Erin cautioned her. "No one can see you."

"Are you crazy?" Addison said but wasn't pushing her hand away.

"To touch your wet pussy and your hard clit, yes."

"Oh, God." Addison's eyes glazed over. "As much as I may want to, we can't do this here."

"Yes, we can. I'm watching, and nobody can see you. Just relax and keep your mouth shut." Erin wasn't going to give Addison a chance to change her mind. She scooted closer and unzipped her jeans.

"You're going to sit there, very still, and I'm going to slide my hand down your pants, through your beautiful, soft hair until I can touch you."

Erin did exactly what she said a second after she described it. Addison's hips jerked into her hand.

"Nobody can see you, and you need to be still or I'm going to stop," she said. She was lying, but she wasn't about to tell Addison that. Erin liked this control.

"Spread your legs for me. Wider. That's good." Erin checked their surroundings again. "No one can see us as I slide my fingers over your clit."

Addison jerked again.

"Be still," Erin said, looking directly into Addison's eyes.

"Fuck you," Addison said teasingly, her jaw clenched, and her eyes filled with lust.

"No. I'm going to fuck you."

Addison moaned quietly and dropped her head back. Erin flicked her clit. She was hard, and Erin knew it wouldn't take much to push her over the edge.

"Shh. You need to be quiet, or I'll have to stop."

Addison's eyes popped open, filled with need. She grabbed Erin's wrist. "You better not."

"It's up to you, Addison, if I keep going."

She saw Addison swallow hard.

"Do you want me to slide my fingers over your clit like this?"

Addison bit her bottom lip.

"Rub you like this?"

Addison nodded quickly.

"How about if I do this?"

"Yes." Addison gasped. "Fuck me."

Addison grabbed Erin's wrist this time to keep it exactly where it was. She let out a quiet moan as she came.

Warmth flooded Erin's hand as she watched Addison climax. She was overwhelmed at the exquisite beauty of the woman before her. Addison's face was flushed, her breathing rapid, her body taut with pleasure. She was absolutely stunning.

"Holy fuck," Addison said, finally able to catch her breath. Her head was still spinning. "In more ways than one," she added.

Not only had she never done anything close to that on a job, but she'd never been finger-fucked with so much intensity it almost blew her head off.

"Yes. It was."

Addison pried open her eyes, and Erin was grinning at her.

"What?" Addison's mouth was dry, but she had no strength to reach for her thermos.

"You are beautiful when you come," Erin said softly.

Addison's stomach flip-flopped at the words and the intensity with which Erin said them.

"Well, you made me that way," Addison managed to say. She desperately wanted to kiss Erin. "Is anyone watching us?"

Sparks flew in Erin's eyes. "No, but they can see me."

"Too bad." Addison leaned over and kissed her. Erin's hand was still in her pants, and the pressure was enough to almost make her come again.

Addison had never felt so content as she closed her eyes for just a moment. The sun was warm on her face, the breeze ruffling her hair, and Erin had her hand between her legs. What more could she ask for? She must've dozed off because she jerked at Erin's voice.

"You better pull yourself together, sweetheart. Our beloved forewoman, Charlotte, is on her way over here."

Addison's head was still spinning as she zipped and buckled up. She tried to look like she hadn't just been finger-fucked into the day after tomorrow, but judging by Charlotte's expression, she failed. She started to get up, but her knees buckled.

Charlotte quickly reached for her. "Are you all right?"

Addison was more embarrassed than anything else. "Yeah. Just got up a little too fast." She looked at Erin, who was grinning widely.

The next week was much of the same, but without dinner and drinks before going to Erin's place. Addison enjoyed following Erin home each evening and left before dawn the following morning. The week after, they managed to eat before reaching for each other, and sometimes they actually made it to the bed before one or both of them came.

The build was coming along nicely, and the interior work was well under way. Addison volunteered to lay the tile in the master bathroom, and her body hummed with the memory of her dream. She told Erin about it that night, and Erin surprised her by suggesting they reenact it the next day in her bathroom. Reality was far superior to her dream.

"I've got a great idea," Addison said one evening as they lay on the couch, naked under a light blanket. The lights were low, and Buoy was asleep on her bed in the corner.

"Takeout?"

Addison laughed. "Let's change roles."

Erin raised her eyebrows, and her eyes flashed. True to her word, Erin did have a toolbox, and they had tried out almost everything that was in it. Addison had never been as adventurous as she was with Erin.

"What do you have in mind?"

"Why don't we spend the night at my place, and you can get up and leave in the morning."

Erin rolled Addison onto her back and kissed her. "I thought you'd never ask."

CHAPTER THIRTEEN

"What is going on between you and Addison?" Susie asked Sunday afternoon. They were in the kitchen, scooping ice cream into plastic bowls. Erin had just made it to her brother's house for burgers after dragging herself out of Addison's bed with just enough time to go home, shower, and drive across town.

"What do you mean?" Erin asked, dodging the question.

"You know exactly what I mean. What is going on between you two?" Susie separated her words for effect.

"What do you think is going on?" Erin asked. What she had with Addison was special. She didn't want to share it with anyone, and she certainly didn't want to have to justify it. They were two consenting adults who knew exactly what they were doing. When Erin thought she had no idea what she was up to, she pushed the thought out of her mind. Addison was leaving in three days, and she was going back to work.

Erin had planned to help with the build for only the first week and then on her days off. But the more time she spent with Addison, the more time she wanted to spend with her. She pulled owner's privilege and took more days off than she'd originally planned.

"Oh, I know what's going on. I want to know what *you* think is going on."

"We're just hanging out and having some fun." We're fucking every chance we get, Erin thought.

"Don't bullshit me, Erin. I've got four kids. I can smell it a mile away."

"Nothing is going on." Erin felt a bright-red sign that spelled out LIAR flickering over her head. They had lunch together every day, and Susie had seen them arrive and leave together.

"Because I love you, I can tell you to pull your head out of your ass and stop hiding behind your flippant, carefree attitude. Something is going on between you two, and the sooner you admit it, the sooner you can do something about it."

"And exactly what would that be?" Erin had been asking herself that same question for days. Maybe Susie would have an answer for her. "I live here, she doesn't. I have a successful business here, and she doesn't live here," she repeated for emphasis.

"So?"

"So?" Erin asked, frustrated. "So, if something was going on, how is it supposed to work?" Her question was not rhetorical.

"You find a way to make it work," Susie said simply. "Do you think everything was laid out perfect with me and your brother? His life was here. My life was in New York. We both happened to be at USC, but that was temporary. We both had concrete plans that did not involve each other. But we loved each other, and we figured out a way to make it work."

"I'm not in…"

Erin stopped. Susie gave her *that* look. Her knees suddenly weak, Erin sat down in one of the chairs around Susie's kitchen table. She was so tired of trying to convince herself that she was not head-over-heels crazy about Addison Bradbury.

"How can that be?" Erin asked, confused, her voice shaky. "It's only been a few weeks. We barely know each other."

Susie put a lid on the pot she was stirring, turned down the burner, and sat across from Erin. She took her hand between her hers.

"Erin, sweetie. You know when you've met the right person. You may not have realized it, but I've seen a change in you. You're calmer, less on edge, and more patient. You have that glow about you that every woman has when she's in love."

Erin breathed in and out several times, starting to panic. "Is it that obvious?"

CHAPTER FOURTEEN

Two days were left before Addison had to return to Phoenix. As always, she was not looking forward to leaving this beautiful island. She loved her job, but it no longer seemed enough. She'd barely thought of Bradbury since she first laid eyes on Erin. Before, Bradbury was always in the front of her mind. Even when she took a few days off, she'd checked her email and kept up with the happenings of her company. But not this trip. Not since she'd met the alluring, fascinating Erin Williams.

They'd been together almost every day for the past two weeks. If they weren't working on the houses, they strolled through the shops in Lahaina and watched the sunset on the beach in front of Addison's room. They talked about everything, Addison telling her about her business struggles, success, and her volunteer program. She mentioned the day she arrived and that she was here for four weeks but had no specific return date. They didn't talk about when Addison would leave.

Addison had "what-if'd" until she couldn't see straight. What if they'd met a different time or place? What if things were different? What if she lived here? What if she had just a job instead of owning a company? What if Erin just worked on a boat instead of owning not one, but two? She was mentally exhausted just thinking about it. Those two words had the biggest impact on her life—what if.

"When is your return flight?"

They were lying in Addison's bed, covered in a sheet of sweat, the curtains billowing in the light breeze. Erin shivered, and Addison pulled up the sheet.

"Day after tomorrow." The word felt like the last day of the world.

"The typical red-eye?"

"Yes. The worst part about coming here is the flight home." Almost all flights back to the mainland left just before midnight.

"The worst part is that you're leaving."

Addison's heart jumped, and she knew Erin felt it. She needed to say something, but what? I don't want to leave, but do I have to? I'm afraid of how I feel about you. Afraid of what I think and how I feel when I'm with you. Afraid of what I'll do without you. Afraid if I walk away, it'll be the biggest regret of my life. Afraid of my answer if you ask me to stay. Afraid of your answer if I ask you to come with me. I'll stay if you ask me to.

Erin was waiting. She hadn't asked a question, but she was waiting for Addison to say something, nonetheless.

"I know."

EPILOGUE

Addison was miserable. The meeting was too long, too boring, and she fought to pay attention. Since returning from Maui she'd been distracted and short-tempered. She tried to hide her feelings, but her staff had noticed, as had her friends. She felt sluggish and out of sorts. She had little interest in her favorite pastimes, no pep in her step, sparkle in her eyes, or any of the other stupid clichés used to describe her behavior. She had once been so focused, dedicated, and completely on while working. She used to look forward to coming to work every day and dreaded the weekends. She lived, ate, and breathed Bradbury. It was her life, and she had wanted it that way. She had no regrets.

The meeting finally came to an end, and she asked her assistant to make sure she had the notes by the end of the day. She'd take them home to read, but they would stay in her briefcase on the floor beside her while she gazed out the window just as she had every night since returning.

Her staff filed in for the next meeting, with Samantha and Cora arriving last. They looked like she felt. Dark circles, drawn, and wrung out. Lyle, Oliver, and Rob had gone last year and came back rested and renewed. What was with this year's trips? The three of them had looked like they wish they had never gone.

Addison half paid attention as each leader gave an overview of the previous quarter's achievements. She faked her way through a few more topics and sent them on her their way. She asked Samantha and Cora to stay behind and took off her reading glasses.

"Why are we so miserable? I know my story. What's yours?" Silence filled the room. "Come on. I know something's up."

The two women looked at each other, probably hoping the other would go first.

"All right. I'll start," Addison finally said. "I met someone in Maui, and she's there and I'm here." It was as simple and complicated as that.

"I met someone in Nassau, and she's there and I'm here," Samantha said.

"I met someone in Jamaica, and she's there and I'm not," Cora echoed.

"Jesus." Addison shook her head. That explained it. "Who would have guessed all three of us would fall for someone unobtainable."

"I'll be fine," Sam said. "It'll just take a while."

"I keep telling myself the same thing," Cora said.

Addison looked around her office at the numerous recognitions and awards people expected to see when they came in. There was the one for the business of the year, the minority-owned company of the year, and the excellence-in-business award, as well as her face on the cover of *Construction* magazine. In this room were her achievements, which she had worked her entire life for. The company she had built had grown into something her father had only imagined. This was her life. And today, sitting around the table with these two extraordinarily strong women, Addison finally understood. This *was* her life. And now she wanted more. She stood up and walked to the door.

"Would you please come in here?" she asked her assistant. "I need you to make three flight reservations for us."

Addison returned to her chair, two sets of eyes on her.

"Where to?" she asked, coming into the office, her pencil poised above her tablet.

"Maui," Addison said, then looked at Samantha.

"Nassau."

"And Jamaica," Cora added, beaming.

Addison turned to face the two women who were more than just employees. They were her friends, and she wanted nothing more than for them to be happy. "Let's go get our girls."

About the Author

Julie Cannon (www.JulieCannon.com) divides her time by being a corporate suit, wife, mom, sister, friend, and writer. Julie and her wife have lived in at least half a dozen states, traveled around the world, and have an unending supply of dedicated friends. And of course, the most important people in their lives are their three kids, #1, Dude, and the Diving Miss Em.

With the release of *Summer Lovin'*, Julie will have twenty-one books published by Bold Strokes Books. Her first novel, *Come and Get Me*, was a finalist for the Golden Crown Literary Society Best Lesbian Romance and Debut Author Awards. Several of her books have additionally been finalists for the GCLS Best Lesbian Romance, and *I Remember* won the GCLS Best Lesbian Romance in 2014. *Rescue Me* and *Wishing on a Dream* were finalists for Best Lesbian Romance from the prestigious Lambda Literary Society.

Books Available From Bold Strokes Books

Flight SQA016 by Amanda Radley. Fastidious airline passenger Olivia Lewis is used to things being a certain way. When her routine is changed by a new, attractive member of the staff, sparks fly. (978-1-63679-045-9)

Home Is Where The Heart Is by Jenny Frame. Can Archie make the countryside her home and give Ash the fairytale romance she desires? Or will the countryside and small village life all be too much for her? (978-1-63555-922-4)

Moving Forward by PJ Trebelhorn. The last person Shelby Ryan expects to be attracted to Iris Calhoun, the sister of the man who killed her wife four years and three thousand miles ago. (978-1-63555-953-8)

Poison Pen by Jean Copeland. Debut author Kendra Blake is finally living her best life until a nasty book review and exposed secrets threaten her promising new romance with aspiring journalist Alison Chatterley. (978-1-63555-849-4)

Seasons for Change by KC Richardson. Love, laughter, and trust develop for Shawn and Morgan throughout the changing seasons of Lake Tahoe. (978-1-63555-882-1)

Summer Lovin' by Julie Cannon. Three different women, three exotic locations, one unforgettable summer. What do you think will happen? (978-1-63555-920-0)

Unbridled by D. Jackson Leigh. A visit to a local stable turns into more than riding lessons between a novel writer and an equestrian with a taste for power play. (978-1-63555-847-0)

VIP by Jackie D. In a town where relationships are forged and shattered by perception, sometimes even love can't change who you really are. (978-1-63555-908-8)

Yearning by Gun Brooke. The sleepy town of Dennamore has an irresistible pull on those who've moved away. The mystery Darian Benson and Samantha Pike uncover will change them forever, but the love they find along the way just might be the key to saving themselves. (978-1-63555-757-2)

A Turn of Fate by Ronica Black. Will Nev and Kinsley finally face their painful past and relent to their powerful, forbidden attraction? Or will facing their past be too much to fight through? (978-1-63555-930-9)

Desires After Dark by MJ Williamz. When her human lover falls deathly ill, Alex, a vampire, must decide which is worse, letting her go or condemning her to everlasting life. (978-1-63555-940-8)

Her Consigliere by Carsen Taite. FBI agent Royal Scott swore an oath to uphold the law, and criminal defense attorney Siobhan Collins pledged her loyalty to the only family she's ever known, but will their love be stronger than the bonds they've vowed to others, or will their competing allegiances tear them apart? (978-1-63555-924-8)

In Our Words: Queer Stories from Black, Indigenous, and People of Color Writers. Stories Selected by Anne Shade and Edited by Victoria Villaseñor. Comprising both the renowned and emerging voices of Black, Indigenous, and People of Color authors, this thoughtfully curated collection of short stories explores the intersection of racial and queer identity. (978-1-63555-936-1)

Measure of Devotion by CF Frizzell. Disguised as her late twin brother, Catherine Samson enters the Civil War to defend the Constitution as a Union soldier, never expecting her life to be altered by a Gettysburg farmer's daughter. (978-1-63555-951-4)

Not Guilty by Brit Ryder. Claire Weaver and Emery Pearson's day jobs clash, even as their desire for each other burns, and a discreet sex-only arrangement is the only option. (978-1-63555-896-8)

Opposites Attract: Butch/Femme Romances by Meghan O'Brien, Aurora Rey & Angie Williams. Sometimes opposites really do attract. Fall in love with these butch/femme romance novellas. (978-1-63555-784-8)

Under Her Influence by Amanda Radley. On their path to #truelove, will Beth and Jemma discover that reality is even better than illusion? (978-1-63555-963-7)

Swift Vengeance by Jean Copeland, Jackie D & Erin Zak. A journalist becomes the subject of her own investigation when sudden strange, violent visions summon her to a summer retreat and into the arms of a killer's possible next victim. (978-1-63555-880-7)

Wasteland by Kristin Keppler & Allisa Bahney. Danielle Clark is fighting against the National Armed Forces and finds peace as a scavenger, until the NAF general's daughter, Katelyn Turner, shows up on her doorstep and brings the fight right back to her. (978-1-63555-935-4)

When In Doubt by VK Powell. Police officer Jeri Wylder thinks she committed a crime in the line of duty but can't remember, until details emerge pointing to a cover-up by those close to her. (978-1-63555-955-2)

A Woman to Treasure by Ali Vali. An ancient scroll isn't the only treasure Levi Montbard finds as she starts her hunt for the truth—all she has to do is prove to Yasmine Hassani that there's more to her than an adventurous soul. (978-1-63555-890-6)

Before. After. Always. by Morgan Lee Miller. Still reeling from her tragic past, Eliza Walsh has sworn off taking risks, until Blake Navarro turns her world right-side up, making her question if falling in love again is worth it. (978-1-63555-845-6)

Bet the Farm by Fiona Riley. Lauren Calloway's luxury real estate sale of the century comes to a screeching halt when dairy farm heiress, and one-night stand, Thea Boudreaux calls her bluff. (978-1-63555-731-2)

Cowgirl by Nance Sparks. The last thing Aren expects is to fall for Carol. Sharing her home is one thing, but sharing her heart means sharing the demons in her past and risking everything to keep Carol safe. (978-1-63555-877-7)

Give In to Me by Elle Spencer. Gabriela Talbot never expected to sleep with her favorite author—certainly not after the scathing review she'd given Whitney Ainsworth's latest book. (978-1-63555-910-1)

Hidden Dreams by Shelley Thrasher. A lethal virus and its resulting vision send Texan Barbara Allan and her lovely guide, Dara, on a journey up Cambodia's Mekong River in search of Barbara's mother's mystifying past. (978-1-63555-856-2)

In the Spotlight by Lesley Davis. For actresses Cole Calder and Eris Whyte, their chance at love runs out fast when a fan's adoration turns to obsession. (978-1-63555-926-2)

Origins by Jen Jensen. Jamis Bachman is pulled into a dangerous mystery that becomes personal when she learns the truth of her origins as a ghost hunter. (978-1-63555-837-1)

Unrivaled by Radclyffe. Zoey Cohen will never accept second place in matters of the heart, even when her rival is a career, and Declan Black has nothing left to give of herself or her heart. (978-1-63679-013-8)

A Fae Tale by Genevieve McCluer. Dovana comes to terms with her changing feelings for her lifelong best friend and fae, Roze. (978-1-63555-918-7)

Accidental Desperados by Lee Lynch. Life is clobbering Berry, Jaudon, and their long romance. The arrival of directionless baby dyke MJ doesn't help. Can they find their passion again—and keep it? (978-1-63555-482-3)

Always Believe by Aimée. Greyson Walsden is pursuing ordination as an Anglican priest. Angela Arlingham doesn't believe in God. Do they follow their vocation or their hearts? (978-1-63555-912-5)

Courage by Jesse J. Thoma. No matter how often Natasha Parsons and Tommy Finch clash on the job, an undeniable attraction simmers just beneath the surface. Can they find the courage to change so love has room to grow? (978-1-63555-802-9)

I Am Chris by R Kent. There's one saving grace to losing everything and moving away. Nobody knows her as Chrissy Taylor. Now Chris can live who he truly is. (978-1-63555-904-0)